More Than Love

The Barrington Billionaires

Book Five

Ruth Cardello

Author Contact

website: RuthCardello.com

email: Minouri@aol.com

Facebook: Author Ruth Cardello

Twitter: RuthieCardello

Goodreads

goodreads.com/author/show/4820876.Ruth_Cardello

Bookbub

bookbub.com/authors/ruth-cardello

New York Times and USA Today bestselling author Ruth Cardello returns with a hilarious addition to Barrington Billionaire series.

What happens when a normally reserved billionaire tries to be a regular guy and discovers he has a wild side? Grant Barrington is a quiet hero who is about to flex his alpha billionaire muscle.

Viviana Sutton is living in Boston after being swindled by her ex-boyfriend. She's done with relationships and isn't looking for forever. Giving in to one naughty, incredibly hot romp with a financially challenged stranger actually makes her feel better until she takes a pregnancy test.

To help his family, he'll need to be the man she makes him feel like he can be.

For the sake of her baby, she'll give him a chance to prove what they had was more than sex—and he's more than just a regular guy.

Copyright

Dedication

This book is dedicated to my friend, Missy. Never stop reaching for your dreams. You are a very talented lady and I'm so glad you're in my life.

My billionaire world at a glance:

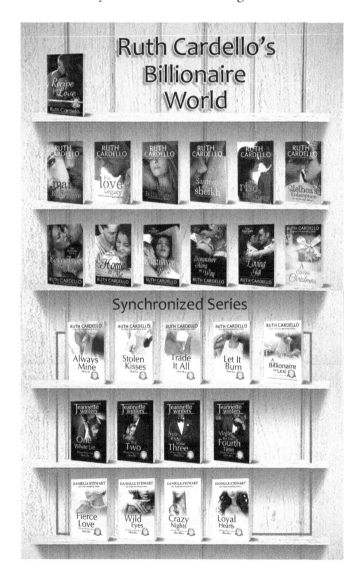

Chapter One

G RANT BARRINGTON'S RIGHT hand tightened on the grip of his Beretta. He brought his other hand around for support then spread his feet shoulder-width apart, bent his knees slightly, raised the gun toward his target, and aligned his sight. Only when he was certain of the shot did he slowly squeeze the trigger with precisely enough force to discharge the weapon.

Perfect shot to a non-kill zone on a paper torso that was moving toward him. He waited before firing again because more than one bullet per second was prohibited. It didn't matter that he was the only shooter on the exclusive country club gun range or that there was virtually no chance that the range safety officer would correct him. Rules and procedures were important. A clean win was the only one worth celebrating.

Another perfect non-kill shot followed by a deadly one to the head just as his retired police captain instructor had designed the drill. Grant's precision brought him little satisfaction. He wasn't practicing to impress anyone. He was a man who believed in being prepared, and this was nothing more than a step in that process.

His brothers joked he was as spontaneous as a sunrise. He took that as a compliment. Reliability was a trait he valued. Once he chose a course, he held to it until he achieved his goal. Perseverance succeeded where brute force failed. Unwavering, methodical action was an under-celebrated, unbeatable force. In a modern culture where the goal was instant gratification and flashy results, Grant remained steadfast to the idea that slow and steady won the race.

He hadn't always been as self-disciplined. When he was still a child, his family was shattered by a tragedy. His mother had fallen apart and his father had lost his fight. None of them had ever been the same. His oldest brother, Asher, had learned to lash out to protect himself. Kenzi and Lance had withdrawn. Ian had become a master negotiator. Each of them had learned to make a life for themselves outside of the family—coming together for a long time only when guilted into doing so.

Grant had found his sanctuary in the predictable nature of numbers and the calm of researching the nuances of financial law. He learned early on information was its own power. Where others fumbled and guessed, he was precise and informed. Not only had he used that skill to stabilize his family's fortune when it had teetered, but he had a reputation for solidifying the prosperity of his clients.

After successfully completing one more drill, he unloaded, cleared and locked the gun, placed it on the shooting bench in front of him, and removed his earmuffs and earplugs. He replaced all of it in his range bag and handed it off to the safety officer. It would be cleaned and ready the next day when he returned. Now it was time for free weights followed by a jog on the treadmill.

"Nice shooting," a man in a charcoal suit with short brown hair said as he walked up. He didn't look comfortable in his suit although it had been tailored to fit him. He appeared close to Grant's age but rough around the edges like someone who had lived a harsher life.

"Thank you," Grant answered with a slight frown. "Do I know you?"

"You might. The name is Marc Stone." He waited for recognition then added, "I work for Dominic Corisi."

It was a questionable reference, but Grant held out his hand in greeting. Although Dominic wasn't someone Grant would count as one of his friends, they navigated the same social circle, and Marc looked familiar. "Nice to meet you. Since it's unlikely you're here by coincidence, what can I do for you?"

Marc shook his hand firmly. "Alethea Niacharos is my fiancée."

Grant looked the other man over again. *Confident. Physically fit. Carries himself like someone with military training. It's plausible.* Alethea hadn't mentioned him, but they hadn't discussed much outside of how to find Clarence Stiles. "Interesting."

"She doesn't know I'm here or that I know the two of you have been in contact. I'd appreciate it if you don't say anything to her."

"I have no reason for further contact with her." Marc wouldn't be the first man to accuse Grant of being with someone he shouldn't have been with, but Grant didn't sleep with married or engaged women. Every single encounter he'd had with Alethea, beautiful as she was, had been purely professional. Anything else would have invited chaos.

"So it's true that you fired her."

"I did. Her investigative skills didn't match my current needs."

"Because she blurs the line when it comes to surveillance laws?"

In an age of easy to conceal cameras and audio recording devices, Grant always chose his words with care. "You would know that better than I, but either way it's no longer of consequence."

Marc rubbed a hand over his forehead. "I wish that were true. I love Alethea, but I'm not blind to her . . . personality quirks. She doesn't respond well to being told she can't do something."

Grant arched an eyebrow. "Then explain to her I didn't refuse her services, I merely invited her to offer them to anyone but me."

Marc almost looked as if he might smile, then he ran his hand over the back of his neck. "I would if I thought it would stop her. The problem is, her instincts are always spot on. This case is frustrating her, and that's not a good sign. Someone went to extreme measures to ensure the truth about your brother's death would stay buried. Your aunt's journal reads like an obituary column, and Alethea thinks you're about to add your name to the list of casualties. I agree. No offence, but you're not exactly the Barrington for this job."

So much for client confidentiality. If Alethea wasn't Marc's source of information, then she was getting sloppy. Someone had loose lips. Rising to his full height, Grant narrowed his eyes. If it had done nothing else, the conversation had supported Grant's instincts to not use Alethea. "Good luck with your fiancée, Mr. Stone." He moved to step around Marc.

Marc blocked his path. "Alethea will be in the mix whether you want her to be or not. She can't help herself. If you're not working with her, that adds another layer to what is already potentially a dangerous situation. Protecting you while hiding from you might be a dangerous distraction for her. I can't let you go forward like this. You have a choice: You can work with her or work with me."

"This conversation is over," Grant said, stepping forward and clipping his shoulder forcefully against Marc's as he passed him.

A second later, Grant was flat on his back, looking into the barrel of a gun, gasping for air as Marc pressed the heel of his shoe into his chest. Another man would have started swearing and threatening Marc, but Grant quickly regained his calm. Anger clouded a person's ability to assess a threat.

If Marc was who he said he was, the only logical goal for knocking Grant off his feet was to scare or confuse him. It was a power move. One of Grant's early martial arts instructors had welcomed each new student with a similar humbling takedown. Grant appreciated Marc's form even as he refused to allow the move to work.

Experience had taught him the best defense for an act of aggression was an equally forceful and unexpected offense. Calculating the necessary leverage and force came naturally. Practiced patience allowed him to give Marc a moment to think he'd won.

Looking confident, Marc lectured, "The people you're hunting won't fight fair. They won't stand perfectly still while you take aim. You need someone watching your back. Am I hired?"

"No." Grant rolled toward Marc, clasped the back of his knee and used his full weight to buckle it. Marc tipped backward, landing on his ass with a thud, as Grant jumped to his feet. After calmly dusting himself off, he held out a hand to assist Marc to his feet.

Marc tucked his gun into a holster beneath his jacket and took Grant's hand. "You'd be dead if I'd wanted you to be," he said once he was on his feet.

"Maybe." He'd never been the type to get in a pissing contest. He preferred the quiet win. Grant glanced around for the safety officer. Although the man wouldn't have the nerve to say something, it didn't mean he wouldn't talk about the exchange once they were gone.

"He's with my men. If they do their job right, he'll think they were here to price membership to the firing range," Marc said.

"I hope they're more subtle than you are." *Henchmen at the country club. Perfect.* Had Grant wanted the drama, he would have let Asher know where he worked out. His older brother had a reputation for being a hammer even when alternate methods were an option. Like Dominic Corisi, Asher had a good share of enemies. And unscrupulous friends. Alethea Niacharos was a prime example, proving that people with similar ethics tended to gravitate toward each other. "Dominic Corisi earned every enemy he has, and I understand why he might require someone like you on his security team. I, however, do not conduct business the way he does. As far as uncovering the truth about a crime that may have occurred nearly thirty years ago, your fiancée's instincts are off this time. It's mostly a paper chase. I won't require anyone to *save my ass*."

"Then why the gun?" Marc asked.

"Insurance, but most likely unnecessary. Statistically, dangerous criminals have shorter life spans. Given the length of time that has passed, everyone involved is probably dead or no longer in positions of influence."

Marc shook his head slowly. "What if you're wrong?"

"I'm not. I've already confirmed what Lance and Andrew discovered in Aruba. There is no proof that Clarence Stiles was involved in my brother's death outside of Andrew's account of their conversation. My brother has had a difficult year. I wish he had spoken to me before involving our mother. I won't know how much Stiles was actually involved until I speak to him myself."

"If finding him was possible, Alethea would have already."

Using a similar tone to what Marc had used earlier, Grant said, "No offense, but hacking into computer systems isn't the only way to locate someone. It's a good place to start, but since her method wasn't productive, it's time for an off-the-grid connection."

"Meaning?"

"I intend to interview every person who ever worked for Stiles, dated him, stood behind him in a grocery line. Someone knows him and knows where he would go. I'll find that person and resolve this."

"Stiles was afraid enough to burn his house with all of the old records in it. A man doesn't do that unless there is still a threat."

Is there anything this man doesn't know? "It doesn't require much of a threat to frighten a coward, but the facts don't match up. Andrew wasn't followed. The private investigator Lance paid to snoop around hasn't encountered resistance. I don't expect to either."

Marc sighed. "Send me. I'll do better at talking to the locals."

"Excuse me?"

Marc motioned at Grant from head to toe. "You reek of money. People won't trust you."

Now that was simply flat-out wrong. "I'll have you know that prime ministers, royal families, and even some dictators trust me with their financial secrets. My ethics are above reproach."

"Yeah, you'll have to tone that way down before anyone on the street will open up to you. What's your favorite beer?"

"I prefer an aged Scotch."

"Sports team?"

"For investment purposes I used to own a hockey team, but the tax benefit from losses wasn't worth the aggravation."

"Hobbies?"

"Never had the time for them."

"Friends?"

"Of course, I have friends." Grant was losing patience with the conversation.

"Any of them not have a trust fund?"

Grant opened his mouth to list those who didn't, but stopped when he realized he couldn't think of any. He'd been born to money, attended private schools before graduating from Wharton School, and worked in the investment industry since. He lived at work, and his clients were people who wanted to stabilize or grow their portfolio rather than start one from scratch. Now that he thought about it, those people weren't what some would call friends—they were a network of business associates he spent time with. That realization was disconcerting and didn't match the image he had of himself. "I don't see how this is relevant."

"Because you're out of touch with reality, and that's a whole other danger. If you're going to do this, you need to get out of the country club and spend some time with regular people."

Regular people. Grant thought about how his brothers, Asher and Lance, had both chosen women from a significantly lower economic stratosphere. *And I like them. I'm not an elitist.*

He reviewed Marc's assessment of him. *But apparently I sound like one.*

"Where do I start?" Asking such a question went against how Grant had been raised. Barringtons didn't need help. They didn't stumble. They didn't bleed. Appearances meant more than the truth. Anything less than perfect had risked upsetting their mother.

That's a moot point now.

His mother was justifiably, unapologetically obsessed with what Stiles had told Andrew because it made possible a memory she'd been told she'd only imagined. She remembered holding Kent, alive and well, after his birth. The doctors had told her that was impossible since Kent had died at birth. Their family, having not been in the room for the birth, had believed the doctors.

Had the doctors lied? It was impossible to ask them since both the nurse and doctor had died within days of Kent's birth.

To cover up what? Negligence? Murder?

His family was scrambling to make sense of the possibility that something horrific, more horrific than a nearly full-term stillbirth, had occurred. If his mother had actually held Kent, then no wonder no amount of counseling had been able to convince her of the opposite. No wonder she'd doubted her own sanity.

Before Stiles claimed responsibility for Kent's death, no one had believed her. No one.

And that had broken her along with their family. In an attempt to protect his wife, their father had demanded an illusion of perfection from his children.

The truth was their road back—and his mother deserved

it, no matter how ugly it was.

"So, I'm hired," Marc said.

"Yes, but with certain conditions." His siblings were all settling down, getting married, and having children. They had too much to lose. His younger brother, Ian, was in town but had gotten a job with the US Embassy in Madrid. A scandal could end his career. "We don't share anything we discover until we are certain of the facts, and if there is danger to my family, we don't come home until we eradicate it. I may not be the Barrington you consider most qualified, but I will do whatever it takes to protect my family."

"Good." Marc nodded slowly. "When are you heading to Aruba?"

"Sunday."

"I won't fly with you, but I'll be there every step of the way. If you see me, I'm doing my job wrong."

"Understood."

"You need an alias. Give me a name, and I'll have IDs made up for you."

"I don't care. Use any name." He snapped his fingers. "Grant E-n-y-n-a-i-m."

"Seriously?" Marc asked.

Grant raised and lowered a shoulder. "You have a better suggestion?"

Marc opened the door. "No. Grant Enynaim it is. I'll be Marc Let's-fucking-come-back-alive."

For the first time that day, Grant smiled. "I want to see that passport."

Marc laughed. "That's funny."

Grant sobered. "Good because if I sound out of touch when I speak, I need to correct that. Instead of working out in the gym tonight I'll jog near the Charles and meet some people. I can't imagine it'll be hard. I'll spend some time with them, listen to how they speak, and have that issue remedied by Sunday."

Marc laughed again then stopped when Grant glared at him. "You're serious. Of course you are."

VIVIANA SUTTON SLOWED her pace so Audrey could catch up. Her friend wasn't out of shape, in fact she had a figure that men jogged backward to take a second look at, but she didn't like to get sweaty. With her hair in a fashionable French braid and her designer spandex, Audrey looked like a bouncy model in a sportswear commercial.

Viviana, on the other hand, was in cotton jogging shorts and a loose, faded T-shirt. She'd tied her hair back without the benefit of a mirror and considered this portion of her daily run, the part where Audrey joined her, her cool down phase.

From the time they were young children, everyone knew Audrey would move to the big city. She was too pretty for a small New England town. Everyone expected her to end up on the big screen in Hollywood or married to some sinfully rich man. She left right after high school but surprised everyone by working for an environmental advocacy agency—saving the world one water source at a time. Living her dream.

She has her life together—me, not so much.

No one ever expected much from me.

Viviana had grown up working for her father's construction and large machinery rental company. She'd commuted to school from home and continued to work for her family after college because her family had needed her.

She didn't consider herself ugly, but she was realistic. Women like her didn't inspire devotion from men. They liked her. She could walk into a bar fight and leave with a new male best friend. She could fish as well as the best of them, parallel park an eighteen-wheeler, and no amount of swearing offended her.

Was it wrong to dream of being irresistible to someone? *No wonder I'm an easy mark.*

"You're not thinking about him again, are you?" Audrey asked.

"Who?" Viviana parried.

"Forget him."

"I can't. What is wrong with me? He didn't even try to sleep with me. That bugs me more than the money he took. Do you realize I haven't had sex with anyone but myself for . . . holy shit, it's been over a year. I'm going to die alone."

"Now you're talking stupid. Let go of who you were in Cairo, New York. Do you know why I moved to Boston? I didn't want to be the person everyone thought I was. I wanted to do me on my own terms. You don't think you're sexy, so men don't see you that way. I'm not actually prettier than you, I just think I am." Audrey's concerned expression took the bite out of her words.

Viviana smiled. *Good try, Audrey.* "No, you are."

"As long as you believe that I always will be. Listen, I'm your friend, and I love you. You pay half the rent so if you want to keep the first job you came across when you moved here and hide out in your room, I'm cool with it. I love having dinner made for me when I come home. I love having someone clean up after me. I wouldn't be a good friend, though, if I didn't tell you that you're not my mother. You don't have to feed me. You don't have to do my laundry. All I want is to see you happy, and I don't think you are."

Viviana sighed. Good friends saw too much. "That stung."

Audrey nodded. "You need a win—something to boost your confidence. You need to pick a man, bring him home, and fuck his brains out. You'll feel better, I promise. Then we'll go get our nails done, maybe have our hair highlighted. We'll have a whole beauty day."

"I think you have it backward. Shouldn't I get the make-over first?"

Audrey threw her hands up in frustration. "No, that's the point. You are beautiful just the way you are. I'll prove it to you. See that guy who just jogged by?"

"What guy?" Viviana scanned ahead of them and her breath caught in her throat. "Oh, that one." Male perfection. Broad shoulders. Tight ass. Muscular legs. If the front of him looked anything like the back of him he was way, way, way out of her league. "What about him?"

"You need to fuck him."

Viviana swallowed hard. "Sure. I bet he's single and has

been waiting his whole life for me."

"If you don't want him, I'll fuck him."

"Do it. I don't care," Viviana said in a terse voice. She didn't expect the shove Audrey gave her.

"Wake up, Viv. This is your chance to recreate yourself and be the woman you want to be. You can do it. Decide you want him and go get him."

"I can't."

"Because you're scared. What's the worst thing that could happen?"

Are we ignoring the possibility that beautiful people can also be crazy psychos? Yes, well, then—"What if he says no?" *And I confirm what I'm already beginning to believe: that I'm universally, sadly quite resistible.*

"What if he does?" Audrey smiled in encouragement. "You'll still be the woman who saw what she wanted and had the courage to go after it. What he says doesn't matter. What you *think* about yourself does. Do you believe a man like that would find you attractive?"

"Maybe?"

"Not good enough."

"Yes?"

"Say it like you mean it."

"Yes."

"That's better. Now, get in front of him somehow."

"Why?"

"So he can see your killer body. You have one, you know. Cut across the corner over there. Get in front of him. Then drop something. He'll stop and help you pick it up.

After that give him some long looks, touch his arm a few times, lean in. You'll know if he's interested."

"I don't know if I can do that."

"How long have we been friends?"

"Forever."

"Trust me?"

"Completely."

"Then go get him, Viv. Remember, this isn't about him—it's about you."

Chapter Two

G RANT WASN'T USED to feeling unsure of himself, but meeting people on the bike path wasn't turning out to be as easy as he'd imagined. Shortly after he'd approached a group of young men and women, they'd bolted with insulting speed. He'd tried to start up a conversation with a man who was picking trash off the grass and was treated to a barrage of profanity simply because he asked if the man enjoyed his job.

Frustrated, Grant had thrown himself into the secondary reason he was there—jogging. His phone rang. He almost let it go to voicemail but decided taking a call from his sister, Kenzi, might improve his mood. "What's up, Kenzi?"

"Game night on Saturday. Are you in?"

"It's a busy weekend. I'm heading out of town on Sunday." Family responsibilities didn't erase the commitments he'd already made to several clients. Luckily a lot of what he did could be done from any location.

"Anywhere exciting?"

"Not really." He didn't want to lie, but he also didn't want Kenzi to worry.

"Drop by in the afternoon at least. Please. Andrew and Helene are up for the weekend. You know how much Mom and Dad love having all of us together."

They do and I can work on the plane. "You win. I'll be there. If I could put in a request, though. Please not charades again."

Kenzi laughed. "Dax said the same thing. I, on the other hand, think it's hilarious to watch you try to look cool while acting out movie titles."

"Yes, well, we have a word for that same experience— torture." He smiled as he spoke, though, because there was a time when every exchange with his family had been strained. Game night had been Asher's wife's suggestion while they were dating, and it had helped to heal his family. A couple times a month he and his siblings gathered at their parents' house and talked about nothing of importance. Impossible as it was to imagine that something so frivolous could achieve anything, game night had brought his family closer together. Considering what his family was dealing with now, that closeness was especially important.

"Emily suggested Bullshit. It's a game where you say what you're discarding but don't show the cards. If someone doesn't believe you they call bullshit, and if you lied you have to pick up the pile."

"So it's a test of how well we lie."

"It's a game, Grant. Children play it. No one is going to judge you for being the world's worst liar—much. I mean, we'll tease you about it, mercilessly probably, but it'll all be in fun."

"Sounds like a good time," Grant said wryly.

"See," Kenzi joked, "a little white lie now and then won't kill you."

I should work on that skill. I'll need the poker face when I introduce myself as Mr. Enynaim. Rather than admitting that, however, he decided to tease his sister. "Have too much fun at my expense, and I'll ask to see your checkbook. Or have you started balancing it since you got married? Maybe that's a question for Dax." Until recently he wouldn't have felt comfortable enough to joke with Kenzi about her husband, but the fabric of his family was changing. Which was one more reason why he chose to be the one to find out what happened to Kent. It needed to be handled just right. Asher would have acted first and thought about the consequences later. Ian would have concealed the truth if he thought it might sully the family name. Neither would have helped his family.

With a light laugh, Kenzi said, "Dax understands my system. I don't need to balance to the penny like some people—ahem—I won't say who. For me, as long as I have a general idea of how much I have I'm fine."

Grant cringed. In the past he would have given her a lengthy lecture on the importance of those pennies and how those who didn't count them tended to lose them, but he didn't. This was an opportunity to imagine what someone who didn't spend their entire day, every day, crunching numbers would say in response. "If that works for you, great."

"Save the sarcasm. I'm not as bad as I used to be. Can we

talk about something else?"

He frowned. *That sounded sarcastic? Dammit. I was shooting for 'I'm cool with it.'* "Sure, what are you—?" He collided with the back of a woman who was crouched down in the middle of what should have been a clear path and momentum carried him over her, unfortunately without the benefit of his feet beneath him. Had he not learned to tuck and roll to break a fall, he would have faceplanted onto the cement. Instead he tumbled several times, finally coming to a rest on his back.

"What the—?" The swear died on his lips when a beautiful, glistening blonde bent over, grabbed his hand and hauled him to his feet before his head had a chance to stop spinning. When she dropped his hand he swayed briefly.

"Oh, my God, I'm so sorry. I wanted to meet—I mean, I dropped my phone, but I couldn't let it fall too hard because I've already had the screen replaced twice. Not that I knew it was going to fall because how could I? Shit, is that *your* phone?" She began rushing around collecting pieces of what had indeed been his phone. "Fuck me. Of course I broke your phone. Perfect. Fucking perfect." She looked at the broken device with the most stunning blue eyes he'd ever seen. "I'm sorry. I don't mean to swear. I do it when I get nervous." She held out his phone to him. "I'll buy you a new phone. Friday, after I get paid. Shit. How much does a phone like that cost? Would they have payment plans?"

"It's insured. No need." He accepted the pieces while studying the woman before him. She was thin, but with more muscle than women he was used to. Her hair was barely contained by an elastic that was off-center on the back of her head. She looked like she cared more about the workout than attracting male admirers, and that was hot. Outside of his family, women in his circle couldn't pass a window or mirror without preening. She was real—raw. *Regular?*

Had he literally run into exactly what he was looking for?

"Thank God because I have maybe twenty bucks in my bank account." She leaned forward and touched one of his temples lightly. "You're bleeding. Fuck. Do you feel okay? Do you want me to call someone? An ambulance?"

He closed his hand over hers and felt a jolt of lust rock through him. *Instead of talking to a regular person, imagine how much I could learn if I spent a weekend fucking one. This one. This perfectly average, unbelievably sexy, hot mess of one.* "Have dinner with me."

She blinked several times fast before answering. "Did you say dinner?"

"Or breakfast," he suggested in what he'd been told was his sexy growl and watched her reaction closely. Did she feel it, too? This—heat? "Or both."

She looked at their linked hands and her mouth rounded in a way that made him want to kiss her right then, right there, before he even knew her name. "You want to have dinner with me?"

"Yes." The look in her eyes told him she wanted the same, and that's all he needed to know.

"It's not every day a woman literally knocks me off my feet."

Her eyes narrowed, and she pulled her hand free. "Ha. Ha."

Focus. What would a beer drinking, sports watching man say to this woman? How blunt would he be? He probably wouldn't follow the three-dates-before-an-orgasm rule of etiquette. Grant stepped closer, and she bit her bottom lip. "Would you be offended if I said you look amazing in those shorts? All I can think about is tearing them off you."

She tipped her head back as he leaned even closer. "Wow."

"Yeah. Wow. Come home with me." *I'm ready to taste some regular.*

A smile spread across her face. She threw her arms around him, but it wasn't the passionate embrace he already fantasized about nearly a dozen times during their short acquaintance. It was the brief, tight hug one friend would give another. "I did it. You would totally have sex with me."

He frowned.

"Audrey was right. I needed a win." She gave him an apologetic smile. "Thank you."

"I don't understand."

Her smile brightened. "I wish I were the type for a one-night stand because I am that grateful. You have no idea how much this means to me."

Another woman slowly jogged by and tipped her head in question.

The blonde before him shot her a thumbs up. "He totally would!"

"Didn't doubt it for a second," the woman called back.

The blonde let out a happy sigh then sobered a little when she looked him over again. "Are you sure you're okay?"

He didn't feel okay. He was turned on and turned upside down. For once in his life he had no idea what was going on or what to possibly say to clear it up. "I must have hit my head harder than I thought, because I'm completely confused."

"Oh"—she chewed her bottom lip—"because I acted like . . . because you thought I would . . . I'm sorry. It was exciting to think I could do it, but I know myself. I can't have sex without being in a relationship, and I don't even know you. Plus my track record lately proves my judgment is way off when it comes to men—"

He pulled her to him then and silenced her with a kiss. It wasn't meant to be a deep kiss, but as soon as his lips touched hers his brain completely shut down and all of his blood headed south. Part of him expected to be smacked. He didn't know her name. What right did he have to kiss her? When her lips parted for him, a primal need surged within him. His body wanted hers in a purely physical, animalistic way. He wanted to carry her off and fuck her in the bushes, in an alley, and he didn't care who watched.

This was a wild side of him he hadn't known existed. Sex had always been good, and he considered himself a considerate lover. It had always been important to him that his partner came first. This was different. His need for the woman in his arms shook him with its intensity. He hadn't realized how cerebral he was during sex until hunger replaced thought. This was the sex he'd heard people joke about but had doubted was real.

I don't care why she tripped me or what she's talking about. I'm going to fuck this woman tonight. All night. And then I'm going to wake up and have her again.

SOME EXPERIENCES WERE life changing. Viviana had felt this way before—the first time she'd tasted expensive chocolate. Well, not exactly this way, but she remembered closing her eyes to better savor the taste and thinking, "Holy shit, so this is what all the fuss is about."

Off to the side of a very public bike path, hungrily kissing a complete stranger, Viviana once again thought: *So this is what all the fuss is about.* She gave herself a moment to savor every unexpectedly decadent sensation.

His kiss was bold and unrestrained. It should have scared her, but instead it called to a side of her that had never been fully satisfied. She'd had tender sex, breakup sex, make-up sex. She'd even once had drunken let's-agree-not-to-talk-about-this-tomorrow friend sex—but she'd never had this. It was as scary as it was wonderful, though. Like a swimmer being knocked off her feet by an ocean wave, if she didn't right herself, it had the power to pull her under.

Bracing her hands to his chest, she pushed back and ended the kiss. Her only consolation as she bent to catch her breath was that he looked just as off balance. When she straightened, they stood there, breathing heavily, looking into each other's eyes.

I should introduce myself. She stuck her hand out. "Viviana Sutton."

He looked down at her hand then back up with a lusty smile on his face. "Grant—Grant Enynaim." His hand closed around hers—strong and sure—just like his kiss.

That touch also ended too soon.

Don't just stare at him—speak. Explain again that what he thinks might happen won't and run. "Well, it was nice to— meet you." She took a step back. "I should try to catch up with my friend."

"Do you like wheatgrass?"

"I don't know what that is." It sounded familiar.

He nodded toward a place behind her. "There's a juice bar across the street. Want to try it?"

Juice bar? That didn't seem like a potentially bad life choice. In fact, it sounded refreshingly healthy. "With you?" *Duh? What is wrong with my brain?* She looked him over slowly. *He's too good looking—that's the problem. I shouldn't talk to him; I should just appreciate the view for a moment more then go before he says something that ruins this memory for me.*

Like: "Hey, I'm married." Or "I only killed a couple of peo-ple—that doesn't make me a serial killer."

He didn't appear to mind that she'd had less awkward conversations with her gynecologist. "No expectations. If it makes you feel better, I'll even let you pay."

Seriously? "You're asking me to join you for a drink that you want me to pay for?"

He seemed to battle with himself before saying, "I didn't bring my wallet with me." Then he smiled and any disap-pointment she'd felt at the idea that he might be more broke than she was melted away. How much could one juice cost?

It couldn't be that much. *And I did break his phone.*

She glanced over her shoulder at the juice bar. Well lit. Busy. *Seems safe enough. Why the hell not?*

Out of the corner of her eye she realized Audrey was lingering and watching. Viviana waved her to go and Audrey did with a huge smile. When she turned back to Grant she caught him watching her and the expression on his face sent a rush of heat through her. Her gaze dropped to his crotch, seeking confirmation before she dared believe he felt the way she did. There it was—an impressively large erection in the front of his jogging shorts. Big and bold just like the man sporting it. *Wheatgrass, huh? Can we roll around naked in it?*

"I don't mind paying," she said in a whispered voice. She raised her eyes to his. The air between them sizzled. She could almost hear her father saying, "A man who makes a woman pay isn't a man she should be with. It's a respect thing."

Being respected is overrated. She shook her head to clear it.

Not that anything is going to happen between us.

I'm not that kind of person.

I hold myself to a high standard of dating someone at least six months before indulging in mediocre, turn-the-lights-off-please sex.

"Great, let's go," he said, placing a hand on the lower curve of her back and guiding her across the bike path and toward the street.

Moments later they were at the counter of the juice bar ordering two shots of what looked like lawn cuttings. A perky teenage girl swiped Viviana's credit card then held out two nasty looking green liquid shots to them. They each took one then stepped off to the side.

Viviana told herself that trying new things was the reason she'd moved to Boston. No one in Cairo served wheatgrass. *I'm here to broaden my experiences. Recreate myself. Maybe this new me loves gross looking health drinks.* "Should we make a toast?"

"We should." He raised his plastic shot cup and said, "To chance encounters."

"To chance encounters," she repeated and tapped her shot cup against his.

He downed his.

She downed hers then made a gagging sound as she thought she felt a piece of grass tickle the back of her throat. "That's quite a drink. You can literally feel how good it must be for you." She wanted to wipe a napkin across her tongue to erase the taste but didn't.

"You hated it," he said, one corner of his mouth curling in a smile.

There was amusement in his eyes and Viviana relaxed a little. *So I don't know him. Isn't everyone a stranger until you take the time to get to know them?* "I'm a strawberry smoothie kind of girl."

He leaned in and ran his thumb over her bottom lip. "It's good to try new things. You can't really say you don't like something until you taste it."

Oh, yes. Viviana followed the path of his thumb with her tongue until she realized what she was doing and watched a flush darken his cheeks. *Holy crap.* As she stood there simply looking up at him, she thought: *Audrey thought he might make me feel better.*

I feel pretty damn good.

Shouldn't I quit while I'm ahead?

"Want to get a table?" he asked.

"Yes," she answered in a breathless tone as she imagined him taking her on it. *Now that is the kind of sex I've always dreamed of—table sex. I've done it on beds. A couch a couple times. I almost did it once in the backseat of a car but I was too paranoid someone would come across us.*

But a table—that's a whole different level.

I bet he has that kind of sex.

He guided her to one near the window. They sat across from each other without speaking at first. She caught a glimpse of herself reflected in the glass and groaned. Her hair was falling out of the elastic she'd tied it back with. Not only did she not have makeup on, but there was also a post workout shine to her face. She tried to discretely tuck some of her hair back in then felt foolish when it sprang free again.

"Let it down," he ordered in a low tone that sent desire licking through her.

She could have refused, but she wanted to make him feel the way she did—completely inappropriately turned on. There was nothing inherently sexy about reaching behind her head and removing the hair tie, but she did it slowly and hoped it looked as sensuous as it felt. His eyes dilated and his nostrils flared slightly when she adjusted her newly freed long curls. Knowing that she had the power to turn him on was exciting.

He ran a hand up her neck and through her curls. When his hand fisted, she arched her head back and parted her lips. Never, never had she felt sexier.

He groaned. "You are . . . unexpectedly irresistible."

Irresistible? Me?

If I'm dreaming, Audrey had better not wake me up.

Me. He craves me.

He bent and brushed his lips lightly over hers. She leaned into the kiss. Location didn't matter. Every inch of her was focused on him and the way she came alive beneath his touch. How much better could this get? *If I walk away without knowing, I will spend the rest of my life wondering: What if?*

"Dangerously so," he added.

It is dangerous. He could be anyone. Is that what makes this so exciting? "I don't do things like this. I don't meet men and dive into kissing them before I know anything about them."

"I don't care if you do."

Ouch. His blunt honesty stung like a slap. She broke physical contact with him by sitting back in her chair.

He watched her closely like a man trying to solve a puzzle. "Would you rather I lie?" he asked in a low growl.

She opened her mouth with a snappy retort but didn't utter it. *What do I want him to say? He respects me?* Sidney had said all the right things and still stolen from her in the end. *He probably thought I had more money than I did.*

It would have saved us both a lot of time and aggravation had we been honest with each other.

So, isn't this better? He's not pretending this will go any-

where. He wants to fuck me. Not make love. Not consummate our feelings for each other through intimacy. Just fuck.

That's awful—isn't it?

It doesn't feel awful.

It feels exactly how he described it—dangerously tempting.

I can't. A wave of disappointment in herself washed over her. *I want more.* "Thank you for the"—she stopped when she remembered that she'd paid for the drinks—"company. I should get going."

"Stay," he said in the same tone that she'd obeyed a few moments earlier, but she didn't let herself succumb to it a second time.

She shook her head, more for her own benefit than his. "I'm working overtime at the office tomorrow morning."

"What do you do?" he asked.

Viviana paused her retreat. He seemed genuinely interested. *And I can be vague.* "I'm an appointment scheduler for a medical center." *Which is technically true.*

"Do you like it?" The simplicity of his question put her at ease. *Maybe it doesn't have to be all or nothing. They could be two people simply getting to know each other. Not dangerous. Not naked. No reason to bolt.*

She shrugged. "It pays the bills. How about you?"

He took long enough to respond that she thought he'd come back with an elaborate lie. "I have a few things in the works."

Yep, I've dated men with that career before. I knew he had a flaw. Men that good-looking don't remain single unless there's something. "I hope one of them comes through for you."

He nodded. "Did you grow up in Boston?"

"No, I just moved here."

"Really. What inspired the move?"

She could have made up a story, but she doubted she'd ever see him again and saying it aloud was freeing. "I wanted a fresh start. I met my ex-boyfriend through my job and that didn't work out well."

"What did he do?"

"How do you know it wasn't me?"

"Just tell me."

"He took my debit card out of my wallet and emptied my bank account before he broke up with me—via a text."

"What an asshole." Grant sat up straight as if preparing to punch someone right then and there. "Did you go to the police? I hope he's rotting in jail."

Viviana grimaced. "I didn't tell anyone. It wasn't worth it."

"Not worth it? He stole your money."

"Fifty bucks." She shrugged, regretting she'd brought the topic up.

"That's all you had in the bank?" The raised pitch of his voice and the real surprise in his eyes was insulting.

Narrowing her eyes, she asked, "Do you know who shouldn't judge me? Someone who mooches drinks off complete strangers."

"I assure you—" He stopped, then said, "You're right."

"I am," she said, feeling uneasy about how easily he'd agreed with her.

"I want to repay you," he said in a serious tone.

"That's not necessary."

"It is." He went to the counter, returned with a pen and wrote a number on a napkin. "This man is a genius when it comes to retirement investment plans. Tell him that Grant sent you."

Viviana reluctantly accepted the napkin. "Thanks, but I'm still operating on the 'paycheck to paycheck, fly by the seat of my pants' system."

"I don't understand."

She raised and lowered one shoulder. "It involves hoping I'm dead before seventy . . . possibly sixty-five."

His mouth dropped open. "You're joking."

She frowned. No matter how hard she'd tried, she had never been good enough for her father or her brothers. The last thing she needed was another judgmental male in her life. To make her point she moved her drink to use the napkin as a coaster. "I'm not."

His eyes narrowed. "Don't be offended. I didn't realize how bad off you are."

"Well, this has been fun." She pulled her hands away from his and stood. Why would God make a man that attractive but that obnoxious? Sick joke?

He rose quickly to his feet. "Don't go. Believe it or not, this is me trying."

"To piss me off?"

"To get to know you. I shouldn't have brought up fi-nances. It's none of my concern."

She sighed. "Technicially, I started it."

"Don't go. How about if I tell you something embarrassing about me then we call it even and start over?"

It would have been a whole lot easier to refuse and walk away if her heart wasn't pounding wildly in her chest simply because he'd stepped closer to her. She folded her arms across her chest. "Okay. Shoot."

"I don't know how to talk to someone I want so badly that I can hardly think around them."

"Oh." Viviana let out a shaky breath. *You're not doing so bad now.*

"So, are we even?" A boyish smile spread across his face.

Even isn't how I would describe how we are. "Sure." Viviana sat back down mostly because her legs had gone wobbly beneath her.

He retook his seat across from her.

"That was really smooth," she said as she took the napkin, wadded it up, and stuffed it in her wheatgrass shot cup. *No way was he getting off the hook that easily.* "Now, cough up an actual embarrassing story."

Chapter Three

GRANT SAT BACK and laughed. His family often accused him of not having a sense of humor. He had never thought too much about it, but perhaps that's who he had become. Decades of being told to be perfect, never be too happy or too sad around the family, had taught him to hold back. It felt good to relax.

That night he didn't want to be a financial wizard. He didn't want to think about the reason that had brought him out to the Charles River. He wanted to simply be a man who was enjoying the company of a beautiful woman. Viviana didn't know who he was. She had no expectations of him, and that was freeing.

Her smile had returned, and he found himself grinning right back. "I can't think of any."

"Try harder." She arched an eyebrow in challenge, and he forgot what she was asking him for. Whatever it was, he wanted to give it to her.

He was momentarily reminded of a similar sensation during a tour through an art museum as a child. His teachers had told him Monet was a talented painter, but he hadn't agreed until he'd seen one of his paintings from across a large room and it had come to life for him. It had ceased to be paint on fabric and had become a feeling he'd never forgotten. Regardless of what happened with Viviana, he knew it would be the same with her. Other women had turned him on, but never like this. He could feel her—every subtle change in her expression, every breath she took, every time she bit her lip nervously. She was gloriously disheveled, and he wanted her so badly he ached.

"Well?" She was also getting adorably impatient.

Oh, yes, she wants a story. He considered admitting where his mind had wandered, but he didn't want to rush getting to know her. He hunted through his memories for a time when he'd been embarrassed. "I've got it. When I was in kindergarten—"

"Seriously? You can't do better than a childhood story?"

"It's a good one." At least he hoped she'd think so.

She cocked her head to the side skeptically. "Okay, I'm willing to hear it, but the jury is still out on whether I accept it or not."

"Fair enough." He chuckled. *Refreshingly hard to impress.* "When I was five years old I fell in love with my first teacher, Mrs. Dube. She wore the prettiest dresses that had buttons from the neckline to the hem. I didn't know why, but I wanted to help her with those buttons so I did the respectable thing and asked her to marry me."

Viviana gasped with amused pleasure. "You didn't."

"I did." He loved the sparkle in Viviana's eyes as she pictured it. "Of course she turned me down. She said I was too young, but I was welcome to ask her again when I was older."

"Oh, that's so sweet. She didn't want to hurt your young pride."

"I thought she simply needed time to think about it. So, the next year, on the first day of school I showed up with my luggage and my mother's engagement ring."

A laugh burst out of Viviana. "No."

"Yes. She explained to me that when she'd said older—she'd meant much older. Then she called my father. I don't know if she would have told him if I hadn't showed up with a real diamond."

"What did your father do?"

"He picked me up from school and took me to the office with him."

"That's it?"

"And he gave me the look."

"The look?"

"It was a disappointed, I-thought-you-knew-better look. Highly effective."

"Really? That's it? You didn't get grounded for taking your mother's ring?"

"My father didn't believe in punishment."

"I can't imagine that. I was grounded all the time."

"So your parents were strict."

"Parent. My mom was sick when I was little. She died when I was eight."

"I'm sorry to hear that."

"It's okay. It was a long time ago. My father raised me

and my two brothers. None of us are in prison, so he did something right."

"That's a low bar to measure success by. Don't you have any aspirations?"

She cocked her head to one side and said, "How do you do it?"

"What?"

She leaned forward and went nose to nose with him. "How do you go back and forth between sounding like a nice person and a complete dick?"

He coughed back a surprised laugh. "I'm working on the latter part."

A reluctant smile tugged at the corner of her mouth. "Well, at least you're aware of the problem. They say that's half the battle."

The *battle* was to not pull her across the table and onto his lap. "I like you, Viviana."

She blushed, and he savored the sheer beauty of it. "I think I like you, too."

He laughed. "You know how to keep a man humble."

"Humble is not exactly how I'd describe you," she joked.

"What's your favorite sports team?" he asked.

"I don't really understand the whole sports fan mentality. I played football in middle school. It was fun, but I wouldn't idolize someone for being good at it."

Grant had never seen himself as someone who was easy to surprise, but he hoped his shock didn't show on his face. "You played football? On a team?"

"Eighth grade. It was a co-ed team—no big deal."

"I've never heard of a co-ed football team."

"Technically my town hadn't either, but I wanted to play. Both of my brothers had and had done well. I needed to prove that having a vagina didn't mean I couldn't catch a ball or outrun a defensive cornerback."

You can tackle me anytime you want.

But football?

He almost said he was surprised her father let her play such a dangerous sport, but he kept that thought to himself. The story intrigued him. "Who were you trying to prove it to?"

"My father." Her expression turned sad briefly, then she said, "I'd rather talk about you. Did you play?"

"No, like you I had brothers who were naturals. I preferred sports that had less chance of residual brain damage. Track and swimming were more my style. I enjoyed setting then beating my own record times."

"That was me in high school. I still have a chart at home where I record my run times."

"Me, too."

"I compare my current times to my best from back then."

He laughed. *Dare I admit it?* "Last year I couldn't match my college sprint time, not even on my best day, so I upped my workouts."

"I have totally done the same. I don't care if someone can outrun me, but I'm damn well going to at least maintain my best. It's about how I feel more than competing with anyone."

"Yes." The more he learned about her, the more he wanted to know. "Because you're still trying to prove something."

"Aren't we all?"

"Maybe." He thought about how he'd turned down the assistance his siblings had offered, telling himself it was better for them if they weren't involved. *Is it really for the best or am I trying to prove something as well?*

"So, you're one of three?" she asked.

"Of five. I also have a younger brother and sister."

"That's a big family. Your poor sister. Four brothers. I can barely handle two."

"You don't get along with your family?"

Her expression sobered again. He regretted asking, but he also wanted to know. Realistically her personal life was none of his business, but a part of him wanted it to be. "I love them." She sighed. "It's just hard. My mother's death changed our family. It changed me. I'm not sure I even know how exactly. It's just a feeling I get sometimes. I think about who I am and who I might have been and I wonder if I've lost part of myself along the way. I came to Boston to try to find out. Does that sound silly?"

"No." He reached out and took her hand in his. No, it didn't sound silly at all. It mirrored how he felt about his own life. "I admire your honesty."

"Life is hard enough without adding a layer of lies to it."

Grant inwardly cringed as he remembered he'd lied about his last name. None of this was supposed to matter. If the conversation led to sex he'd thought names wouldn't matter in the face of a hot memory. He hadn't expected to feel anything for her—certainly not the protectiveness that was battling with the part of him that kept imagining how good it would feel to kiss his way up those beautiful thighs of hers. "Viviana, my real—"

Her phone beeped with a message pulling her attention away from him. "It's Audrey. She's checking if I'm okay." She shook her head, typed something back, then stood and said, "I should get going."

He rose to his feet. "Of course." He didn't want the evening to end, but they were both in workout clothing and unless he asked her to go home with him there weren't too many places he could think of taking her. Still, the lure to find a way to stay together was undeniable. If the yearning he saw in her eyes was anything to go by, she felt the same way. "I'll walk you out."

She motioned toward a hallway toward the back of the juice bar. "I need to use the restroom first."

"I'll wait," he said.

"You don't have to." After a brief pause she said, "That would be nice."

VIVIANA THREW A paper towel into the trash bin beside the sink and studied her expression in the mirror. There was a glow to her cheeks and a sparkle in her eyes. Her hair was disheveled and wilder than normal, perfectly matching how she felt.

He makes me feel beautiful.
And sexy.

But I'm neither. At least, I've never seen myself that way.

Viviana had lied to Grant. Audrey hadn't texted to see if she was safe; she'd dared her to take it all the way. "Just do it," Audrey had said. "You'll see yourself differently tomorrow."

That's what I'm afraid of. I don't even know who I am anymore. How could doing something impulsive help now?

She'd followed her first instinct and ended her time with Grant. *Because hiding instead of overcoming my insecurities is what I do.* As she faced herself in the mirror, she admitted that many of her choices had been in response to something she was afraid of rather than a journey toward her own dreams.

A memory, one that had shaped so much of who she was, fought to surface, but she pushed it back. *It doesn't matter who said what anymore. I'll be twenty-eight on my next birthday. It's time to stop blaming others for who I am and start taking responsibility.*

She glared at her own reflection. *I don't like you.*

She sighed. *I want to.*

How do I get to a place where I do?

Audrey says I need a win in the form of a good ole fashioned mind-blowing fuck. I would argue that she's wrong, but since that doesn't describe any of the sex I've ever had—I really don't know.

Even Grant said you can't say you don't like something until you taste it. Taste. Lick. Nibble on. It all sounds good.

What's the worst-case scenario? I go home with him, have disappointing sex, and discover one-night stands are not my style.

At least it'd give my vibrator a night off.

Or I could continue to hide in here until I admit I'm acting juvenile and essentially demolish what little remains of my self-esteem.

I may be overthinking this mindless, exciting sex stuff.
Fuck.

Viviana turned away from her reflection. *If I run away from this, what am I running back to? I left Cairo because I wanted more, but I'm slowly recreating my safe, boring existence here.*

It doesn't have to be perfect. Isn't that what Audrey was saying? Who he turns out to be doesn't matter as much as what I prove about myself.

Boston is about me—discovering who I am.

And tonight maybe that means a dare and a stranger.

Whether he says yes or turns me down.

No matter what the sex is like—I refuse to sit back and hope my life gets better.

I'm doing this.

Viviana threw open the door. It crashed against the wall with such force that Grant appeared, looking concerned.

"Are you okay?" he asked.

Barely breathing, she looked him in the eye and said, "Please fuck me." She closed her eyes briefly as her request echoed in her own ears. *Really smooth.*

When the world didn't end, she tentatively opened one eye to check his reaction. His expression gave little away so she opened both and looked lower. His response was hard, huge and straining against the material of his jogging shorts.

With her heart beating wildly in her chest, she searched his face again.

"Come here," he said in a husky voice that was a caress of its own.

She almost did as he asked, wanting nothing more than to give herself over to the desire pulsing through her, but instead held her ground. This was her fantasy and it would happen on her terms. "You come here."

He didn't immediately move, and she began to mentally flog herself. *I could have played it cool. I could have flirted and gotten at least a dinner before he broke it to me that I'm not really his type. What kind of woman blurts out—*

He stepped closer and a slow, lusty smile spread across his face. "Only because you said please."

"I didn't—oh."

I did.

She licked her bottom lip and ran a hand boldly up his muscular chest. His heart was beating as wildly as hers. She was tempted to tell him again that this wasn't how she normally behaved. She didn't want to talk, though. She wanted to feel. With a move she'd never before dared, she cupped the back of his neck and met his kiss halfway.

He pulled her against him, against his excitement, and plundered her mouth like a long separated lover returning with an insatiable hunger. It was everything and more than she'd imagined.

A stranger shouldn't taste as good as he did. His touch shouldn't feel as right. Location ceased to matter. She soared to a place where each caress made her want more. More teasing tongue play, more of his bare skin against hers.

She was vaguely aware of him lifting her so she straddled his waist. The ease with which he carried her made her feel wantonly feminine. She desperately wanted him and how he made her feel to go on.

Letting the sensuality of it all lead her, she moved her sex back and forth over his pulsing cock and dug her hands into his hair. If she could bring him even half the pleasure he was bringing her . . .

The wall behind her fell away—or was it a door? Without breaking their kiss, Grant stepped through it, closing it behind him. Her shoulders hit the wall with a thud, and she groaned with pleasure.

In moves as bold and confident as the man she was writhing against, Grant whipped her shirt up over her head and dropped it to the floor. He removed her sports bra with an impatience that Viviana wholeheartedly approved. Once freed, her breasts were his to ravish, and he did.

She threw her head back and held on to his shoulders while he roughly kissed one then the other. There was no tenderness in his touch, but Viviana didn't want there to be. When his teeth grazed over her nipple she called out his name and almost came right then. She dug her nails through the fabric of his shirt and into his back. When she thought it could get no better, he shifted her weight more against the wall and slid his fingers up the leg of her shorts and beneath her panties.

She was wet and ready. His fingers were talented and un-restrained. His thumb settled over her clit, rubbing back and forth against it while his middle finger dipped inside her. All while he suckled and teased her nipples. In and out, back and forth. He set a rhythm that rocked through her.

She came with a sob that brought his lips back to hers. Still shaking and coming down from an orgasm that put all past ones to shame, she found herself being lowered back to her feet. Had she been capable of speech she would have begged for him not to end it there. No, something that wonderful couldn't be so short-lived.

He pulled her shorts and panties to her ankles. She stepped out of them and almost fainted when he dropped to his knees and threw one of her legs over his shoulder. She fell back against the wall and braced herself with her arms as his tongue loved her. She'd always thought oral was a nice way to gear up for sex, but this was an experience all its own. He parted her, teased her, then fucked her with his tongue. She closed her eyes and prayed no one could hear the cries of pleasure she couldn't hold back.

When she was once again writhing and begging him not to stop, he did, and she thought she would die—or kill him. As he stood, she frantically reached for him. He pulled the waistband of his shorts down and freed his cock. She was so hungry for him, she dropped to her knees without hesitation and took him deeply in her mouth. All she wanted, all she craved, was to bring him the pleasure he'd brought her. Normally she worried about technique or if the man would tell her when he was about to come, but this time all Viviana cared about was how good he felt. She bobbed up and down on him then cupped his balls and licked each one of them before taking his cock into her mouth again.

There was a sweet perfection to it.

She ran a hand up his rock-hard thigh and behind to grip his ass. He fisted his hands in her hair and groaned, but didn't come.

Instead he called her name and hauled her back to her feet. There was a brutality to the move that matched how primal their mating was, and she loved it. His mouth closed on hers again and the taste of that kiss was a mingling of them on the most intimate of levels.

His hands closed on her hips and this time when he lifted her it was to hover her above the tip of his cock. She wrapped her legs around his waist and cried out her need to feel him. Her words were lost in their heated kiss, but he knew what she wanted.

He backed her against the wall and thrust up into her powerfully, burying himself fully in her, then withdrew and drove himself into her again. She hung on, opening herself to him the best she could, and loving the feeling of being claimed. Because that was what he was doing. This was not a man making love to a woman. This was one animal claiming another—as basal as it got—fucking at its purest form. No apologies. No hesitations.

As they moved together, they found a rhythm. She met his thrusts with her own. It was no longer a plundering as much as it was a wild mating. In that moment, regardless of who they were to each other—he was hers and she was his.

She was so blinded by the intensity of her own orgasm, she couldn't say if he came. She assumed he did because he gave a final deep thrust and groaned as she melted against him.

Coming back to earth was not as fun as soaring off to heaven. Slowly, she became aware that, still in her running shoes, she was naked and wrapped around a stranger in what looked like a small storage closet. With his cock still buried within her, he kissed her neck and she shivered.

Wrong had never felt so right.

"Oh, my God," he said.

Ditto.

He slowly, tenderly withdrew and lowered her to her feet. For a moment he looked as bewildered by what they'd done as she felt. When he glanced down to adjust his shorts, he swore. "I didn't use a condom. I always use one. I'm sorry. I don't know what I was thinking."

"It's okay," she said even though it was far from okay. She'd always had an erratic cycle and had been told that conceiving might be impossible for her. But in the age of transmittable everything, that probably wasn't his first concern.

I'm such an idiot. Teenagers have unplanned, unprotected sex. Adults don't. Not responsible ones, anyway.

I know what he was thinking, because I was right there with him the whole way.

Wild, mind-blowing sex.

I should have asked Audrey what people say to each other afterward.

He bent to retrieve her clothing and handed it to her in true gentlemanly form. She accepted it without meeting his eyes and dressed quickly.

"That was amazing," he said softly.

"Yeah, I—uh—we—yeah."

"Are you ready?"

She raised her eyes to his. "For?"

"For me to open the door? It's probably better if no one finds us in here."

"Oh. Yes." She smoothed her hair because it was as out of control as she felt.

He guided her out of the closet and into the hallway with the same calm confidence he'd shown earlier. Was he the same on the inside or, like her, were his thoughts ricocheting? There was something surreal about walking beside him back into the main area of the juice bar as if nothing had just happened. *As if everything I thought I knew about myself hadn't just been turned upside down.*

He stopped at the counter and asked the attendant for a pen and a piece of paper. A moment later he turned to her and smiled. "You can't leave without giving me your number."

My number. Oh, yes, because men call after encounters like this—never. She considered giving him the phone number of her favorite Chinese restaurant, but didn't. *I just fucked a complete stranger in a storage closet and loved every minute of it. I can either second-guess everything he says or I can ride this out. He wants my number.* She took the paper and wrote her real number on it. *Fine. He may be the kind of man who asks but never calls, but I am no longer a woman who is ashamed of her sexuality.*

Call me. Don't call me. It doesn't change what I've proven to myself.

I wanted you.

I had you.

I'm not a passenger in life anymore. I'm fucking driving.

I'm fucking driving.

As she handed the paper back to him, she said, "Thank you." And meant it. Not only had it been wild and spontaneous, but it had lived up to the fantasy. How often does anyone get to say that?

He cocked his head to one side as if she were a difficult to solve puzzle. "I don't know you well enough to take you home, but I hate to end the night like this."

"Can I have my pen back?" the cashier asked, saving Viviana from having to respond.

Grant returned it to her then guided Viviana out of the juice bar and onto the sidewalk. "I want you to know that—"

"Don't." She leaned forward, went up onto her toes, and kissed him briefly. There was a decentness about him that she empathized with. Was it his first closet romp, too? What difference would it make if it were? The chance that she would ever see him again was slim to none. Rather than ending the night awkwardly, she'd prefer they both walked away smiling. "I had a great time."

He nodded and blinked several times. "I did, too."

She used her phone to summon a car to pick her up. Luckily one was right around the corner. "It was nice to meet you, Grant Enynaim."

He opened his mouth to say something, but the car

pulled up beside them. In place of words, he kissed her deeply, hungrily, then dropped his arms. "I'll call you tomorrow."

Her body warmed and revved for him, but she shook her head and opened the car door. No etiquette course was required to know their time together had come to an end. "Goodnight, Grant." She told the driver her address and closed the door.

As soon as the car pulled away from the sidewalk, Viviana laid her head against the seat and closed her eyes. She didn't look back to see if he was watching her go.

Maybe it's better if he doesn't call.

Not every person who comes into your life is meant to stay.

Audrey was still out when Viviana arrived at their apartment, which was perfect because it allowed Viviana to head straight for the shower. She scrubbed herself down more thoroughly than normal while reminding herself that she'd done nothing to be ashamed of.

I'm an adult.

He's an adult.

Sex happens.

Shame is learned—and subjective. I will not succumb to it.

And yet she lathered, scrubbed, rinsed, and repeated several more times beneath the hot spray. After she turned off the water and wrapped herself in a large white towel, she sat back against the sink counter and took a few deep, calming breaths.

Audrey would say—

It doesn't matter what she would say because I'm not

Audrey. I'm not completely fine with what I did. But that's okay, right?

Because this is my journey.

I am not a one-night-stand-with-a-stranger kind of woman. There, I said it. It was exciting and the best sex I've had to date, but I don't like the aftertaste.

And that's okay, too.

I know what I want now and what I don't.

She smiled and wiped a piece of mirror so she could see herself. The woman who looked back at her was complicated and confused, but she wasn't scared anymore. *I'm done apologizing for being me.*

What's that trite saying? You have to like yourself before anyone else will like you. Well, I've taken the first step in that journey.

I followed my heart tonight—okay, my groin if we're going to be precise—and it took courage. If I apply that courage to other areas of my life I'll start applying for those jobs I was sure wouldn't hire me and stop avoiding phone calls from my family because I don't want to answer their questions.

If I can fuck a stranger in a storage closet, I can tell my father I schedule donor deliveries for a sperm bank. It's not like I assist in the process.

Viviana smiled at her own joke, knowing it was one she would never utter in front of her family. As far as her father and brothers knew she was the oldest living virgin on the planet and she was pretty sure they'd kill anyone who came forward with proof of the opposite.

She gathered her things and took them to her bedroom.

She placed her phone on her nightstand then sat on the edge of her bed and frowned at it. Bolstering her ego, she said aloud, "If you don't call me it's your loss, because I am so much more fun than I thought."

Chapter Four

T HE NEXT DAY, Grant did something unusual, he decided
to drive his LaFerrari Spider instead of utilizing his usual
driver and the Bentley. The sports car had been stored in his
garage since he'd received it as a gift a year ago, driven only
enough to maintain it. It was over the top powerful, sleek,
and flashy—everything Grant normally gave little value.
He'd intended to hang onto it for a polite amount of time
and then either donate it for tax purposes or private auction
it for a profit. But that day he wanted to drive something
that reflected how he felt, and to do that he'd chosen a car
with—swagger. He was pretty pleased with himself as he
drove to his parents' home.

*Not the Barrington for the job? Too predictable? Too bor-
ing?*

I fucked a woman in a juice bar storage closet and nailed it.

*I might fuck another complete stranger tonight simply be-
cause I can. I knew I had a wild side and last night proved it.*

*There is nothing my brothers have done that I couldn't have,
had I wanted to.*

When he stopped for a traffic light a beautiful brunette

walked in front of his car. She paused, looked over the car, then him, and winked. His smile widened. *I would fuck her if she were taller and blonde.*

At the next light the window of the car next to him rolled down and a business card flew through his window and onto his lap. A blonde woman with an undeniably stunning rack blew him a kiss and motioned for him to call her. *I would fuck her if her hair were longer, and she had the kind of smile that's impossible not to kiss.*

Like Viviana's.

He revved the engine and sped down the street, several miles over the speed limit. As he drove he made mental inventory of the single women in his life. From his secretary to his dental hygienist, he allowed himself the luxury of imagining being with each of them.

It was a surprisingly disappointing fantasy thread. He sat in his car in front of his parents' and mulled why. How could he have discovered the sexual animal within him and not want to unleash it again?

He took out the piece of paper he'd tucked into his wallet. *Viviana's number.* Common sense told him not to call the woman he'd lied to about his identity and then had sex with within hours of meeting. There was nowhere good that could go.

He closed his eyes and remembered the feel of her lips on his cock. Heaven. Every taste of her, every way they connected, flashed in his mind until he was sporting a painful boner the likes of which no man should have while sitting in his parents' driveway.

I don't want my secretary or some woman I could meet at a bar tonight. I want more of last night—more of her.

Shit.

On the new cell phone his assistant had delivered that morning, Grant typed in the number of the woman he'd spent the evening with, telling himself he shouldn't see her again. He held his breath and shifted uncomfortably in his seat while waiting for her to answer.

"Hello?" Her voice was as sweet as he remembered.

"It's Grant. Grant from last night. At the juice bar." He laid his head on the steering wheel briefly. *I sound like an idiot.*

"Oh, hi. I didn't think you'd actually call."

"I wasn't going to." *Fuck. Did I need to say that?*

"Well, okay, you're honest at least . . . I guess that's a good thing."

Not as honest as you think. Part of him wanted to blurt out his real name and apologize right then. Another part of him, possibly the part that was tenting his pants, wasn't ready to do anything that might kill his chance to be with her again. "I want to see you tonight."

"Tonight?"

"I have a family commitment during the day, but I'll be free around dinner."

"Are you married?"

"No."

"Would you tell me if you were?"

The question took him off guard, and he laughed. "Yes, but if I were the type to lie about being married then I would also likely be the type to lie about lying so my denial doesn't prove much."

There was a pause. "So you *are* married?"

I need to shut up until some of the blood heads north to my brain again. "No, I'm extremely single."

"I'm not sure what that means either."

"It means I can't stop thinking about you. I want to take you out tonight then take you somewhere where we can do everything we did last night—but slower—better—again and again. I want to make you come so many times you beg me to stop then beg for more."

The door of his parents' house opened and his mother waved for him to come in. He raised a finger in the air, requesting one more moment. His father joined his mother on the steps and Grant's dick had never been more conflicted. "Say yes," he ordered in a strangled voice.

"Yes," she whispered, and he nearly came in his pants.

"I have to go. I'll text you when I'm done here."

"I work until four."

"That's easier. I'll pick you up at your place at six."

"How do you know—oh, you heard me tell the driver. I don't mind meeting you somewhere."

Was that what she was used to? Men who didn't bother to pick her up at her home? He could be that man if it meant she would continue to see him as she had the night before. Just an ordinary man.

Wealth a blessing and a curse when it came to dating. The more zeros a man had in his net worth, the easier it was to find female companionship. The difficult part was knowing that some were more attracted to his money than they were to him.

Some pretended not to be, but when he took them out they wanted to be on display. He didn't doubt that many of them would have pandered to almost any fetish he claimed to have, but for the wrong reasons. If he wanted to buy that kind of sex he would have hired an escort, but he never had. For him, there was nothing sexy about fucking someone who wanted his wallet more than his cock.

Viviana was different. She had no idea who he was, and yet she'd wanted him every bit as much as he'd wanted her. With her it was raw and real—and addictive.

How could he not want one more day of that?

As he thought about what kind of date he would have planned if he were a man with very little money, he decided he liked the idea of meeting her somewhere. Where would a man take a woman if he couldn't afford much? "I'll meet you at Quincy Market at six. We can get a sandwich or something."

"On me?" she joked.

He smiled as he remembered that she'd bought the drinks at the juice bar. She probably thought he'd arrive without his wallet again. *And yet she said yes.* His heart thudded loudly. "How about if I pay for dinner and you buy dessert? Have you tried the cannoli at Carol Ann's Bake Shop? They're as good as—I hear they're as good as anything you could get in Italy."

"Sounds nice. I'll see you there at six."

"Yes. I'll text you when I arrive."

"Okay. Bye."

"Bye."

After hanging up, Grant took a moment to savor the afterglow. *No, I'm not being entirely honest with her, but if things work out I'm sure she'll forgive me for being filthy rich. I've never met a woman who had a problem with it.*

He looked down at his still semi-erect cock. *Calm down so we can go in the house. Don't make this awkward.*

His oldest brother, Asher, held his young son up to knock on the window of his car and Grant's problem quickly disappeared. He opened the car door and stepped out. His nephew, Joseph, had grown considerably in the short amount of time since he'd seen him. Before too long he'd be speaking. "We were about to head in but Mom was worried that something was going on with you. Everything okay?"

"Of course," Grant answered. Joseph opened and closed his hands at Grant in a motion that meant he wanted to be held. Grant accepted him with the ease of an uncle who had not only held him many times but had also changed his diaper a time or two. Emily, Asher's wife, had joked that he'd handled the first mess with less drama than her husband had. The compliment had not come as a surprise. Grant tended to handle every crisis, major or minor, with less fanfare than his older brother. "What a big man you are. And so heavy." He pretended to drop him. Joseph giggled. Asher didn't. It was almost comical to see his normally overconfident brother hover like a new mother.

Emily joined them and whistled appreciatively. "Nice car."

Asher frowned at the sports car then gave Grant a long, assessing look. "Where's your suit?"

Grant shrugged. "I felt like wearing jeans today."

Asher made a speculative sound deep in his throat.

Emily laughed. "Grant, that's his way of saying you look nice."

Grant smiled and gave his sister-in-law a kiss on the cheek. "Emily, you don't have to translate Asher for me. I know what he's thinking, but I'm in too good of a mood for it to bother me." He tickled Joseph's stomach, making him giggle again. "Who's your coolest uncle? You know it's me."

Andrew pulled in and parked his car behind Grant's. He waved then walked around to open the door for his fiancée, Helene. Hand in hand the two headed over, and it was a sight that warmed Grant's heart. Not too long ago the family had worried they'd lost Andrew. No one had been able to break through his PTSD to reach him—until Helene. She'd won over the entire family when she'd brought him back into their lives. Grant felt as protective of her as he did his younger sister, Kenzi, and that was another reason he'd taken on the role of family detective. He would uncover the truth, and he hoped when he did it painted her uncle in a better light. Stiles had said he was responsible for Kent's death, but what that meant was purely speculation. If there was even the slightest good in what her uncle had done, Grant would uncover it for Helene's sake.

Andrew gave Asher a loud crack of a pat on the back then turned his attention to little Joseph. "What are you feeding your kid, Asher? I swear he doubled in size."

Asher smiled with pride as if the growth of his child were by his command. "He'll be tossing footballs with me before long."

Grant lowered his voice and stage whispered, "Don't worry, Joe, I'll talk to your mom about how all that head cracking leads to brain damage. There's still hope for you." Then he turned to Helene. "How is that African elephant doing?"

A bright smile lit Helene's face. "Good. She's settled in and they've already introduced her to her herd. We were right there to help with the transition." She hugged Andrew's arm. "I am so grateful to be a part of it this time and to have Andrew to share it with."

Andrew pulled her to his chest and kissed her forehead. The look of love on his face was so pure, so unfiltered, that Grant cleared his throat and blinked a few times as emotion took him by surprise. As he searched for how he'd lost one brother, the reality of how close he'd come to losing a second was unsettling.

Whatever the truth was about Kent, Grant wouldn't let it threaten the life Andrew was making for himself. *Not on my watch.*

The insertion of questionably clean fingers into his mouth brought Grant's attention back to Joseph. He pulled the little hand out and looked around for a napkin. Emily held one out to him, but when he released the imp's hand to reach for it, Joseph solved the problem by wiping his hand on Grant's T-shirt. "Okay then," Grant said and laughed, tossing the napkin back to Emily. "I guess I don't need that after all."

Andrew laughed along then slugged Grant in the arm. "Hey, have you been working out?"

Since middle school, and we probably bench press the same amount. "Have you been showering? I'm not getting the full zoo aroma," Grant joked instead.

There was no use trying to convince his brothers he wasn't a nerd who hid behind a desk all day. They had an opinion of him that he'd cemented in high school by participating in international chess competitions. Back then it hadn't been about the win as much as studying the strategies of the greatest at the game. More than once Grant had let an opponent who needed the cash prize win. He knew his trust fund balance to the penny and could not in good conscience let another man leave the table without the prize if he needed the money. When Grant threw a match, he did it so well no one was the wiser—he was that good. His brothers had never understood how he could enjoy something he wasn't the best in. How could he lose—publicly—and not feel badly about it? Grant didn't bother to try to explain it to them. It would have been like talking to a lion about deciding to go vegan.

Perhaps because their father, Dale, had suffered such a public loss with his career—his brothers didn't back down. They refused to come in second place. It had been too difficult for any of them to attend any of Grant's matches once they weren't sure of the outcome. They didn't understand when the collateral damage would have been too high, the loss *was* a win.

Andrew lifted Joseph out of Grant's arms. "You don't

mind if I smell like a zebra now and then, do you? Do you?" He tucked Joseph against his side and asked the group in general, "Is Lance coming today? I haven't seen Wendy and Laney since they came home from the hospital. How is he surviving all that estrogen in his house?"

Before anyone could answer, another car pulled into the driveway. Kenzi and her husband, Dax. Behind them came an SUV with Lance, his wife Willa, and their month-old babies, Wendy and Laney. Ian arrived as they were still unloading.

"Looks like we're all here," Grant said.

"Are you coming in or should I have lunch served out there?" his mother called from the doorway, but she was smiling. Over the last two years the family had multiplied and each new addition brought them closer to being the family they always should have been.

"We're coming, Mom," Kenzi called out between hugging everyone. Dax was at her side, smiling and shaking hands. Kenzi couldn't have chosen a better, more loving husband, but he wasn't comfortable with physical displays of affection.

Normally Grant felt the same, but that day he decided to fuck with him just because he could. He walked over and gave him a good, back-thumping hug. "Good to see you, Dax."

Dax stood immobile, neither refusing nor accepting the action. When Grant stepped back, the cautious look of concern on Dax's face was priceless. "Good to see you, too, Grant."

Kenzi completely misread the exchange and beamed a smile at both of them. "It really is good to be together, isn't it? I know we're all busy, but when we get together it's worth it."

Looking frazzled and tired, Lance and Willa joined them, both balancing baby carriers, diaper bags, and an assortment of toys. Grant swooped in to relieve Willa of little Laney as well as the heavy diaper bag. He nodded for Ian to do the same for Lance and wasn't surprised when Ian chose the toys and bags over the baby. None of them had been around babies much before Joseph was born and Ian still wasn't comfortable around even him. He didn't like surprises or messes, and Joseph was a constant supplier of both. Grant didn't tolerate chaos in his workplace or his checkbook, but the kind of trouble Joseph brought wasn't trouble at all. After all, what investment was more valuable than the next generation? "Hello, little Laney. You look more like your mother every day. Beautiful."

Willa laughed and sighed. "Not feeling too beautiful yet. I told Lance we didn't need a nanny, but if these two don't start sleeping on the same schedule I may change my mind."

With baby carrier still in hand, Lance pulled his wife in for a quick kiss. "And you say you want more."

Willa's huge smile didn't falter. "At least two more. I've always wanted a big family."

"Me, too," Emily added and hugged Asher.

"Oh, boy," Asher joked, but the look he gave his wife was one of love and agreement.

One of the house staff arrived with a tray of hors

d'oeuvres.

Ian laughed. "Dad's getting itchy in there—we should go in before we're all in deep shit."

Joseph clapped his hands and said, "It. It. It."

"He's beginning to repeat everything. You have to be careful." Emily wagged a finger at Ian, who instantly looked contrite. Regardless of how much power Ian wielded in the political world, he was intelligent enough to bow to a mama bear.

Asher laughed. "You do not want to be the one who taught him his first swear. The second maybe, but not the first."

Emily glared at her husband, and he stopped smiling even though he looked like he still wanted to. "Not funny."

Asher tipped his head to one side and gave his wife a strategically imploring look. "Not even a little?"

She sighed.

He snapped his fingers and true delight lit his eyes. "You swore in front of him, didn't you?"

Emily blushed then narrowed her eyes. Although she didn't look upset, it was obvious she was a little embarrassed by the public reveal.

Grant shot Asher a look that his older brother surprised him by not only correctly interpreting but also acting upon. Asher's expression softened and he hugged Emily. "I tease only because on your worst day you're a saint compared to me. I don't deserve you, but you're stuck with me." He nuzzled her cheek.

She blushed for an entirely different reason, and Grant

nodded with approval before reminding everyone they needed to go inside. They were making their way in when their parents met them at the bottom of the steps.

"I'm sorry, I couldn't wait another minute to see my grandbabies." His mother cooed at each of them in turn then smiled at her children. "You don't know how happy it makes me to see you all together."

His father's attention was on his wife's smiling face, then the babies, then his children. From Asher to Kenzi, there had never been a doubt that Sophie was Dale's first priority. It was something even Grant had resented when he was younger. Grant didn't think he'd ever understand the choices his father had made. By giving Sophie's mental health priority above the needs of his children he had gutted their family even more than the loss of Kent had.

Was he even aware of the role he'd played in their underlying dysfunction?

Grant half hoped he wasn't. Regardless of the mistakes he'd made, there was no denying Dale had suffered right along with his wife. First with the loss of their child, then with the near loss of Sophie. Since Grant had never faced such a situation himself, he admitted he didn't know if he could have done better. He liked to think he would have, but isn't that what every child thinks? That they can do better than their parents? How perfect the world would be if things actually worked out that way.

As they all made their way into the house, Kenzi exclaimed, "I wasn't thinking about Joseph when I chose the game for today."

Willa inserted, "I've heard that children call it Baloney."

Kenzi dug a playful elbow into Grant's side. "Are you ready to lose?"

Grant grinned. He felt too good to throw a game that day, and it was time for some of his siblings to eat a little humble pie. He bent so only Kenzi could hear and said, "Prepare to have your ass kicked."

Eyes wide, Kenzi laughed. "What is with you today?"

"I'm in a good mood. Is that so shocking?"

Narrowing her eyes, Kenzi said, "I realized yesterday there were two charges in my checking account that I don't remember making."

Grant shrugged. "I'm sure you'll figure it out."

She grabbed him by the arm and brought him to a halt. "Okay, spill it. Where is Grant, and what have you done with him? The car. The clothes. The jokes. What's going on?"

Dax leaned in and said, "There's only one thing that puts a look like that on a man's face."

Grant didn't deny it, and his grin widened.

Kenzi's mouth dropped open. "You met someone? When were you going to tell us?"

"It's not like that," Grant denied quickly.

"Like what? Serious? You're not getting any younger. It's time to start considering reassessing your standards."

"Oh, I have." There might have been a little devil in his grin because Dax laughed.

"What is so funny?" Kenzi asked as she planted her hands on her hips.

Dax wrapped an arm around Kenzi's waist and pulled her to him. "I don't think you want to know, Kenzi, and I'm pretty sure you'll never meet her."

Grant nodded in agreement, but didn't like how he felt after he'd done so. Kenzi looked as disappointed as Grant felt in himself. He might not imagine a future with Viviana, but she wasn't a joke to him either. He wanted to back the conversation up, tell Dax he was wrong and that—what? How exactly was what he was doing different than what Dax was imagining?

Luckily, there wasn't much time to mull those questions. A few minutes later his family was gathered around a table, swapping stories and laughing while they ate.

After lunch they played Baloney and Grant dominated the silly card game. With the snoozing infant, Wendy, cuddled to his chest he straight-faced lied about the piles of cards he laid down with such conviction that his siblings could only wildly guess. They were on the last round when he finally let his mind wander to where he was headed afterward.

He thought about what Dax had said about there being a low likelihood Kenzi would ever meet her, and it made him wonder how she would mix with his family. Once they got over the shock of him bringing a woman home, they might actually like her. She was quick-witted and funny, but there was also a strength to her they'd respect.

All his mother would have to hear would be that she'd lost her own mother at a young age and she'd practically be adopted right then and there. His brothers had all chosen women with heart and integrity over pedigree and wealth, so unless she acted like a complete asshole they would accept her.

As he listened to his brothers banter back and forth, he wondered how Viviana was with her brothers. He smiled as he decided she would definitely hold her own.

After he finally announced he had somewhere he needed to be and said his goodbyes, Ian pulled him aside. "I heard you have business out of the country. Aruba?"

"Yes."

"Have you learned anything new?"

"Nothing I haven't already told you. Stiles was careful not to leave a hackable trail. No emails. No money transfers. Nothing. It's impossible to find him from here, but I will find him."

Ian grimaced. "I'm half hoping you don't. Do we really want to know what happened? Kent's dead. Mom already runs to the phone every time it rings like she's going to hear good news. We have to be realistic. What you're going to find out, if you locate Stiles, is how he died. Helene is good for Andrew; the wrong news could threaten what they have."

"It won't." Grant understood what Ian was saying: The truth was important unless it had the power to destroy them. "And I'll be discreet."

Ian ran a hand through his hair and loosened his tie. "I know you will be. If Asher were going I'd be lining up lawyers and media contacts. You know that something like this has to be handled delicately."

Even though they agreed, Grant needed to make something clear. "I will tell Mom the truth—no matter how ugly it is. She deserves that much."

"Of course, but talk to me first. The truth can be spun—"

Grant shook his head. "Not this truth, Ian. I can promise I won't say a thing I'm not absolutely certain of, but I won't pretty it up. The last thing Mom needs now is another lie."

"I wasn't suggesting—"

"Yes, you were." As Grant spoke he realized he was being a bit of a hypocrite, but he pushed that thought back because the last thing he wanted to feel when he saw Viviana again was guilt. He glanced at his watch. Time to go. "I'll call you when I know something."

Ian laid a hand on his shoulder. "Tell me if you need anything."

"I've got this," Grant said, but he was touched by Ian's offer of help. In the past, his siblings had felt as uncomfortable offering help as asking for it. Things truly were changing for the better.

"I know," Ian said and stepped back.

Grant was already in a good mood, but his heart started racing as he headed for his car. He'd ditch it back at his house, freshen up, pick up some condoms, and taxi over to meet Viviana. He revved the engine and peeled out, more excited about seeing her again than he would have admitted to anyone.

A short time later he was on his way to her. He took advantage of the time in the cab to search for the perfect place to spend the night with her. He couldn't take her back to his penthouse or he'd have some explaining to do. She had a roommate, and he didn't want to be rushed or quiet. Something simple. Not the five-star hotel or private home rental he would normally have chosen.

He searched the Internet for cheap, clean hotels and found a new one in the Boston area. *Hours and Yours* was a pop-up hotel the travel sites said was big with millennials. The rooms were small, modern, and could be rented by the hour or by the night. Check-in and checkout was managed by mobile device, and the door opened with a code that was sent via text. He scanned photos of the room and became aroused when he saw the one with bunk beds and a metal ladder. The kind of sex he wanted to have with her could benefit from such props.

Would she let him tie her to those rails? The ladder lent endless possibilities for intriguing positions. How could a man not smile with a night like that looming? The taxi driver gave him an odd look when they arrived at Faneuil Hall, and he threw money at him and jumped out like a teenager meeting his first date.

I'm here, he texted.

Me, too, she answered. **In front of the street performer. He's not bad.**

Grant scanned the crowd until he located her then closed the distance with long strides. She didn't move from her spot, but her eyes widened. "Hi," she said softly.

He couldn't help himself. He cupped her head and pulled her in for a deep kiss. He didn't care who was around or what they thought. One taste. One touch and he was on fire. When he finally raised his head they were both breathing raggedly. "Hi yourself."

She smiled shyly, and he wanted to kiss her again so badly he could hardly think. "Hungry?" she asked.

Her gaze slid from his mouth to skim his chest and lower. That was all it took for his cock to vote they skip dinner and find that hotel . . . any secluded area would do. He didn't care. Grant had the strength, however, to stick to his original plan. "I am, but we have all night."

She bit her bottom lip and flushed. "I need you to know I've never done what we did. Never."

He leaned down to whisper in her ear. "Good, I hope you say that again after tonight."

Her mouth formed a surprised circle. "I—I—"

He kissed her neck, loving how she arched it for him, then kissed his way up her jaw to near her ear again. "Trust me."

Her hands gripped his shoulders and she shook with desire as he kissed his way back down her neck. "How can I when I don't know you?"

He raised his head. "You will." He knew in that instant one more night with her would not be enough. He didn't know where they were headed, but since he was sure mauling her in public wasn't the best way to gain her trust, he straightened and took her hand in his. "Let's go have our first date."

VIVIANA STRUGGLED TO gain control of her traitorous libido while being led through the large indoor market. *Can you have a first date with someone you've already had sex with?*

His hold on her hand was confident and strong. For a man who might not have a job, he carried himself like someone who owned the building they were walking into. He wasn't cocky, but he definitely had a presence that made people instinctively step out of his way—even the young and normally irreverent. Boston was known as a college city. Saturdays brought out the students as well as families.

As far as first dates went, Quincy Market wasn't a bad choice. The main part of the building was wall-to-wall food vendors selling some of the best food in the city. The outer glass areas housed individually run "wagons" where one could buy crafts, jewelry, or touristy items.

Viviana expected Grant to rush her through the merchandise area, but he did the opposite. He stood beside her, asking her about the items she showed interest in. At one point she was convinced he was about to offer to buy her the cheap costume jewelry set she'd playfully tried on, but he hadn't. He'd instead asked her if diamonds were her favorite gem.

She'd wrinkled her nose. "I'm not really the diamond type."

"There's a type?"

She'd replaced the jewelry in its box and said, "They're for women with closets full of dresses who care about the name brand of their shoes." She'd waved her tennis shoe clad foot at him. "I'm more comfortable in jeans and these."

He'd looked her over slowly, appreciatively, then said, "You'd be beautiful in anything, but if you don't like dresses, you've never owned the right one."

"I guess." He had a way of phrasing things that sent her thoughts instantly to the gutter. The way he said owned filled her mind with memories of how good it had felt to be taken by him. There was something primal about their connection. She'd never wanted to be owned by anyone, but if she did, it'd be by someone who made her feel the way he did. "Maybe I'll find that dress one day."

He'd smiled then. She indulged in a brief fantasy of him saying he'd buy her that dress. She'd refuse of course. *I wouldn't accept a gift like that.*

But it's nice to dream of being offered.

"For now, how about getting a quick bite?" he asked.

Now that's more my style. "Seafood?" she asked.

"Love it."

"Lobster roll?"

"My favorite."

She smiled. "Me, too."

He pulled her close and kissed her forehead. "Mayo?"

She shuddered. "Butter."

"Yes. I like to taste the lobster and not someone's secret sauce."

"I said that just the other day."

His smile widened. "I didn't expect to have so much in common with you."

She looked down at their linked hands then back at his face, mulling his admission as she did. "Is that a compliment or an insult?"

He gave her a lingering kiss that erased any doubts his words had birthed. "It's merely the truth. Speaking of the truth, were you trying to meet me when you dropped your phone on the path?"

Viviana's cheeks warmed. "A lady doesn't plot and tell."

He threw back his head and laughed. "Of course not, how uncouth of me. Well, whatever brought us together, I'm glad it did."

"Me, too," she said softly. She hadn't told Audrey where she was going because she wasn't ready to answer any questions about it.

Earlier that day Audrey had asked her if she'd gone home with Grant, and Viviana had answered honestly, "No." She hadn't. She didn't tell her friend about the closet because, although she wasn't ashamed of what she'd done, she wasn't proud of it.

If this date with Grant led to another she'd tell Audrey the whole story. If not, then it was probably for the best. Some memories, even ones as hot as those she hoped to have by morning, were better when they didn't include an attempt to justify them.

What she was doing with Grant wasn't wrong.

It wasn't right, either.

But she'd waited her whole life to feel the kind of passion and pleasure she'd experienced with him. Who could walk away without one more taste?

With a condom this time. She'd stuffed several in her purse before she'd left her apartment.

Once they had their rolls and drinks, they sat at one of the tables in the middle of the building. And they talked. For hours.

He described his siblings although only in the most general of ways. She described what it was like to be raised by a burly father and two meathead brothers. Normally when she met a new man she toned down that part of her life. It didn't put Grant off. He seemed genuinely interested.

Maybe because she was determined to keep her expectations low when it came to where this relationship was headed, she wasn't afraid to be herself with him. Could hearing that she liked to fish lower his opinion of her? She was pretty sure he didn't give a shit about that side of her. And it was freeing.

The third glass of cheap wine they were sharing helped, too.

"I woke up one day and realized I didn't want to be the person I had become." She shook her head. "I came to Boston hoping to find another side of myself. I'm still working on it."

"How old are you?" he asked.

"Twenty-seven."

He nodded. "You have time to figure it out."

She swirled her wine around the bottom of a clear plastic tumbler. "It's hard to find yourself when you're with people who see you only one way. My claim to fame in high school was that I had arm wrestled and beaten most of the boys in my class," she said.

He laughed, leaned forward, and placed his arm on the table between them. "Show me how."

She loved that he didn't doubt her. Nor did he mock her. She stood and took her power stance. "First put your right foot forward and under the table."

Grant stood and did just that.

"I wouldn't tell my opponent the next part, but if I put my thumb under my fingers when I clasp your hand it'll give me an advantage later."

"I'll pretend I don't notice." He clasped his hand around hers.

"Then I lean into the table so I can use it as leverage. What I lack in arm strength I'll make up for by using my core muscles."

"And again this is something your opponent wouldn't expect."

"Exactly."

"The key is to keep your arm close to your body."

"Got it."

"The next part is all about surprise. If I can bend your wrist forward it'll weaken your grip. Your attention will go there. Then I use leverage to compensate for the strength difference. If I'm fast and you don't know the move, your arm will hit the table before you've figured out how to counter." With their hands clasped on the center of the small table and their stances in battle-ready form, she asked, "Do you want to try it?"

He seemed to consider it. "You've already given away your advantage."

"Yes, but you could test the technique now that you know it."

"You wouldn't care that I'd win?"

"We're not in competition with each other—are we?"

He smiled and used his thumb to caress the inside of her wrist. "No, we're not. So, tell me, what did you need to prove in high school?"

She was only beginning to unravel that herself now. "I don't know. That I was worthy? That I could take care of myself?"

"Your brothers didn't protect you? From the way you describe them they sound like the type who would."

"It's complicated." She went to pull her hand away, but he held it there.

"So uncomplicate it. Remove the emotion and give me the facts."

She looked away before raising her eyes to his again. "I've never told anyone. I'm not the whiny, crying, weak type who gushes on about the past."

"No, you're not, but there is nothing inherently wrong with a good cry. Who told you there was?"

To answer him honestly she needed to face a secret shame she'd carried with her for a long time. Voicing it felt like a betrayal. "My father is good man."

Grant's hand tightened on hers. "But?"

She sat and he followed suit. Memories came surging forward and she clung to his hand as she was transported back in time. "I was devastated when my mother died. She was sick for a long time, but that didn't make it easier. I cried so much at her funeral that my father walked away from me. He walked away from everyone. One of my uncles followed after him and so did I. I was so afraid to lose him, too. I hid behind a tree. He didn't know I was there. He wouldn't have ever said anything to hurt me. But I heard him say he wished they'd stopped at two children. He asked my uncle if he thought it would be best to place me with his sister. Boys were different, he said. They were easy. He didn't know what to do with me. I didn't realize it until I left Cairo, but I spent almost the next twenty years trying to prove to him that I was not a problem—that I was as capable, smart, and strong as my brothers. I love my father and my brothers, but I've never told them what I heard that day. Talking about it would hurt my father, and I know he loves me. In my head I know he didn't mean what he said that day. He didn't send me away." Viviana didn't need to wipe away tears because she'd taught herself not to cry. "I don't want to be angry about something that happened so long ago, and I don't want to let it control me anymore. I'm on a journey to find me, and I'm hoping that Boston is where that happens." She sighed with relief. Voicing what she'd held in for so long released her from the weight of it.

"Thanks for sharing that with me. You truly are a re-markable woman." He leaned forward and kissed her gently, a move that was almost her undoing. "Was last night part of that journey?"

She smiled. "Maybe." She laced her fingers with his. "You're a bad influence on me."

He kissed her knuckles. "So bad I'm good, I hope."

She had trouble maintaining eye contact as she admitted, "I wouldn't be here now if you weren't."

His expression turned serious. "I should have been more careful last night. That won't happen again. I'm prepared tonight."

"I share equal responsibility. I am, too."

His eyebrows rose. "You are?"

"I'm a grown woman. I can stop at a pharmacy and buy condoms. Anyone who can't has no business having sex in the first place."

"I couldn't agree more." He leaned forward again and asked softly, "How many did you bring?"

"Excuse me?" she asked with a surprised laugh.

"I'm curious."

She glanced at her purse. "I'm not sure. I didn't exactly count them."

A lusty smile spread across his face. "I did, but since your number is unknown let's play a game." There it was—the tone he used that shot desire through her, warming her skin and wetting her panties.

"What kind of game?"

"The one with the most condoms wins."

She laughed, all tension from before forgotten. "Wins what?"

"Whatever they want tonight."

Oh, yes.

Oh, no. This requires some ground rules. "As long as it's something the other person is comfortable with."

"Of course."

Viviana reached for her purse then glanced around. "Right here?"

Grant answered without hesitation. "I don't care if you don't care." He wiggled his eyebrows. "Unless you're embarrassed by how many you brought."

She unzipped her bag. "I don't embarrass that easily. Prepare to go down."

He wiggled his eyebrows again. "That's one option. I'll decide after I win."

His playful smile tugged at her heart. For a brief second she wished they had started differently. She wondered how she would have felt in that moment if this stage had come later—layered on something solid.

Stop. She warned herself. *If I can't appreciate this for the simplicity of what it is, then I should go home now.*

He's not making promises or professing feelings.

I'm not expecting this to end with a proposal.

I like how I feel when I'm with him, and I'm beginning to like who I see in the mirror. He is helping me find a path back to myself. Maybe that's all this was meant to be.

And if so—isn't it still pretty damn amazing?

She removed a foiled condom from her bag and placed it on the table between them. "One. Match it or lose."

He made a show of reading the packaging. "Extra large. I'm flattered." Then he dug into the front pocket of his jeans and placed one of his own similar condoms then added another. "I match your one and raise you one."

He looked so damn proud of himself she grabbed the front of his shirt and pulled him across the table for a deep, lingering kiss. With her lips still hovering close to his, she murmured, "Two is conservative. Realistic." She sat back, lined up a second condom next to his and added an additional one. "However, I can match that and raise you one."

He chuckled. "I see we share the same optimism about tonight." He ran a caressing hand down her neck and over her arm before reaching back into his front pocket. "I match your three and raise you another."

The sound of a slap drew Viviana's attention away from their game. A passing couple had paused and were momentarily taken in by the scene before them. At any other time, with any other man, Viviana would have been mortified, but with Grant she felt young, sexy, and shameless. She smiled at the couple and said, "Seven should be enough, don't you think?"

The couple looked shocked to be included in something so intimate. They nodded and retreated. Viviana burst out laughing.

Chapter Five

GRANT LAUGHED SO hard his side cramped. Never. Never had he met a woman he enjoyed being with as much as Viviana. She was a delightful combination of shy and bold, soft and strong, sincere but also sassy. He had no idea what she would say or do next, but he wanted to be there to experience it.

Of course she could win an arm wrestling match. He loved the idea of her taking on the entire male population of her high school one at a time—and winning.

He didn't like the reason behind why she'd done it, but her ability to look back at what her father had said with sympathy and loyalty touched him deeply. Viviana Sutton was a good person. He wished he could have spared her from the pain she must have felt when she'd heard her father wished her gone, but he was old enough to understand that with pain came growth. Her decision to move to Boston was a reasonable one. He didn't know why she'd only had fifty dollars for that douche she'd dated to steal, but the more he learned about her the less he believed it was because she was irresponsible. It wasn't something he could ask her about without offending her, so for now it was on the backburner.

As he reflected on all she'd shared about her own family, he regretted that he'd restricted himself to names and ages. She had opened up to him with such heartfelt honesty that he'd again been tempted to tell her the truth. If he did, and she didn't run off angrily, she'd see how much they had in common.

Loss had changed both of their families. He'd lost a brother. She'd lost a mother. Both families had struggled, stumbled, and were dealing with the aftermath. *I know how it feels to hold my tongue because there is no winner when it comes to loss. Everyone suffers. Everyone makes mistakes and does their best to piece things back together.*

I could tell her now.

Or I can tell her tomorrow.

It wasn't simply the promise of a night of sex with her that he wasn't ready to risk losing. Things would change the second she knew he was rich. She'd look at him differently—in a better or worse light. Money and power were two things that very rarely brought out the best in a person.

Would she be more careful around him? Suddenly see him as a fish she could lure in?

Or watch what she said because she thought he would be critical only because he had more.

She might become insecure . . . or defensive.

Whatever her reaction, he would bet his trust fund it would change how they were with each other. *I'm not ready to lose this yet.*

I want more of her.

More of being just the man who wants her. No explanations. No pressure. Just us and how we make each other feel.

He scooped up the condoms, pocketed them, then began to gather their trash from the table. "Ready to get out of here?"

She let out a shaky breath, but nodded. "Where do you want to go?"

He considered taking her straight back to the hotel, but this was a date. Yes, a cheap one, but he wanted to do it right. "There's a bar down the street that is supposed to be good. I heard they have darts. I've always wanted to try it. Want to give it a go, or are you already a pro?"

She visibly relaxed. "I am awful at darts, but I enjoy it. Let's do it."

He returned after depositing their plates and glasses in the trash and held out his arm for her to take. "Cannoli for the walk?"

"I thought you'd forgotten about dessert," she joked as she looped her arm through his.

"How could I when *you're* buying?" he parried back then brushed his lips gently over hers and started walking with her toward Carol Ann's. She smiled between their kisses, and he was glad he hadn't said anything.

Just a little more time like this. Then I'll tell her.

A few minutes later, after sharing one decadently delicious cannoli and making their way to the nearby bar, they took a seat at a high top table and waited for their turn on the dart board.

"You didn't win, you know," she said as she looked over

the drink menu. "I still have some left in my purse."

A waitress came over and took their drink order before he had a chance to answer, but once they were alone again, he said, "I suppose it depends on my definition of winning. I'll gladly concede to you if it means I get to give you what you want."

Her eyes darkened with a look he already knew well. When her lips parted it was frighteningly easy to forget what they were talking about. Part of him was kicking himself for taking her to a bar before the hotel. Another part, though, wanted to be right where he was, taking the time to enjoy getting to know her before he enjoyed her body again.

"Have you ever been incarcerated?" she asked.

I didn't see that question coming. "No, you?" He held his breath, hoping she didn't reveal something that would change how he saw her.

She laughed. "Of course not."

He accepted the domestic beer the waitress delivered and took a sip as he mulled why she thought he might have been. To his surprise the brew was refreshing, earthy, just like her. He took another sip before asking, "Then why do you think I may have been?"

She sipped at her own beer and took a moment before she answered. "You're too perfect. There has to be something wrong with you."

"I've been thinking the same about you."

The shy smile she gave him was adorable. "You don't have to say that. I'm a walking disaster most of the time."

"Are you? That's not how I see you."

She cupped her glass with both hands and spun it slowly before raising her eyes to his. "How do you see me?"

There was uncertainty mixed with hope in her eyes, and it called to his protective nature. He hated every man who had said or done something to make her doubt herself the way she did. "I see a strong woman who has decided to live her life on her terms and to not settle for the hand life dealt her." He reached across the table and laced his fingers with hers. "A woman I didn't expect to enjoy as much as I do. You are not only sexy as all hell, but you're also fun to be with." There was an awkward pause after his declaration, as if he'd said too much too soon.

A young man placed darts on their table and said, "We're done so it's all yours."

"Thank you," Grant said. He offered a hand to Viviana. "I'll let you go first to show me how it's done."

"Okay," she said as she picked up one of the sets of darts. "But I'm not very good."

"I'm sure you're fine."

The first dart missed the board entirely and stuck in the dark paneled wood beside it. Her second landed on the floor below, falling far short of the mark. She cracked her fingers, rolled her shoulders and squinted at the board. While holding one dart shoulder height she glanced back at Grant. "Do you mind if I take a step closer?"

For the safety of the other patrons he did not. "No, go ahead."

"The dot in the middle is a bullseye. That's what I'm aiming for." She did a couple of test moves with her arm.

Just as she was about to let it fly the waitress asked if they were all set and she turned to answer her, a miscalculation that sent the dart soaring about six feet to the left of the board. It landed near the foot of a very large and very drunk looking man.

With a roar the man rose to his feet and stomped over. "You're fucking lucky it missed me," he yelled at Viviana.

Grant stepped in front of Viviana, which brought him toe to toe with a man who towered over both of them like some Neanderthal throwback. "It was an accident."

"They'll call what I do to your face an accident if you don't back the fuck up."

Grant took a step back only because there was no reasoning with drunk and angry. "You're overreacting because you're intoxicated. Nothing actually happened."

"I don't like the way you're looking at me," the bear of a man growled.

"Why don't you go back and sit down?" Grant suggested.

"Why don't you shut the—?" The man swung a fist at Grant that was pathetically easy to dodge.

"I don't want to fight you," Grant said. He felt a little sorry for the man and whatever had brought him to this place in his life.

The man took another swing that Grant again easily dodged.

"Stop now before you get hurt," Grant said firmly.

Rather than helping the other man gain control of himself, Grant's warning seemed to push the man over the edge.

He charged at Grant, but he did so in such a sloppy manner that a simple leg sweep sent the drunk man crashing to the floor.

"I'm going to kill you," the man said as he pushed himself off the floor and back onto his feet.

Grant looked around with mild irritation. "Don't bars like this have bouncers?"

The drunk charged again, and Grant raised his fist and stopped him in his tracks with a controlled punch to the face. The man sank to his knees with a bloody nose. Grant used one of the napkins from their table to wipe a spot of blood from his knuckles. He turned to check on Viviana, hoping the scene hadn't upset her. Outside of the fact that her eyes were huge and round, she seemed fine. As the man on the floor swore loudly and struggled to his knees, Grant said, "I'm sorry. I thought this place would be safer. Let's go."

Viviana nodded, still not saying anything.

Grant tossed several bills down on the table and on impulse picked up his set of darts. He half turned toward the dart board and let the first fly. It hit dead center. The second did as well.

He had the third poised and ready to throw when the drunk took a step in their direction again. He aligned his sight and it whizzed by the man's head so closely it scared him.

Grant said, "I'm sorry. I'm still learning the game."

The other man ran his hand over the side of his face as if expecting to find a cut. "You're both fucking crazy," the man said before turning away from them and stumbling back to his friends.

"Ready to go?" Grant asked, holding his arm out for Viviana to take.

Viviana blinked a few times then linked her arm with his. "I can't decide if I'm scared now or totally turned on."

He let out a hearty laugh as they made their way out of the bar. "I'm the one who should be scared. Please tell me you don't own a gun."

She wrinkled her nose at him, then swatted his chest. "I am slightly nearsighted."

"Really, I never would have guessed."

She glared at him but he kept smiling until her expression softened and she started to laugh, too. "Why do I find you attractive again?"

They'd just stepped out onto the sidewalk when she asked. He spun her, backed her against the outside wall of the bar, and kissed her until she was wild in his arms. Then, and only then, did he raise his head and ask, "Because I'm close enough for you to see?"

Her head was tipped back and her breathing was as ragged as his. "Yes, that's it."

They both shared a brief laugh then he took her by the hand and hailed a taxi. "Let's go."

A FEW MINUTES later they were in a taxi speeding off to a hotel Viviana had never heard of. Cuddled against Grant, with her head on his shoulder, she had to remind herself she'd just met him the day before. Shouldn't it take months to feel so comfortable with another person? She thought about the men she'd dated for much longer and never felt this at ease with.

This has to be something special, doesn't it? Nothing could feel this good and be meaningless, could it?

Unable to answer the questions that plagued her, Viviana pushed them aside. *Some things just need to play out.*

"I can't believe you got a hotel room," she murmured against his neck.

"I can't believe it was only fifty bucks," he said with a proud-of-himself look that made her think he wasn't joking.

He must be. "I would have brought an overnight bag had I known."

"It also rents by the hour so we don't have to stay."

See, he's joking. People aren't serious when they say stuff like that. "Ha ha," she said, but her confidence started to dip when they pulled up to a tall brick building flanked by a sports store and a hot wings restaurant. She sat up and looked from him to the hotel and back to him.

Hours and Yours.

Hours.

He's actually taking me to a hotel room that is rented by the hour.

Is this better or worse than a storage closet?

He paid the taxi driver then took her hand and led her through the front door of the hotel. In place of a receptionist there was a security guard. *Classy.*

"Don't we need to check in?" she asked as her gut flipped nervously.

He took out his phone. "I checked in online. I have a room number and the code to open the door. Efficient and cheap. You can't ask for better than that."

"Efficient and cheap. That's one way to describe it."

When they reached the elevator his expression turned concerned. "You hate it."

Her opinion of the hotel no longer mattered; she saw disappointment in his eyes when she didn't immediately correct him. *This might be the best he can afford. Does it matter how much he spent as long as we're together in it?*

Doing this. She framed his face with her hands and kissed him hungrily.

His arms were around her, lifting her so he could kiss her more deeply. They fell back against the wall and rolled together, neither caring when the elevator door opened and closed beside them. Maybe someone came out of it or maybe not. Maybe someone was there watching them or maybe they were alone. Nothing mattered more than the touch and taste of each other.

Between fevered kisses they made it up to their room, through the door, and fumbled to turn on enough lighting so they wouldn't trip as they navigated their way to the bed. Viviana was lost to the passion of the moment. She tore his shirt off and made quick work of his jeans. This time she wanted him as bare to her as she'd been to him.

He yanked off her clothing with the same wild haste. His lips grazed each new area he exposed. Her hands hungrily caressed every inch of him. He backed her up until her legs met the edge of the bed. She brought a hand out to steady herself and made contact with a ladder.

She froze.

A ladder?

When his mouth closed around her nipple and his tongue began its magical circling she ceased caring why there shouldn't be a ladder in their room. His hand traced her stomach then cupped her sex possessively, and she threw her head back, gripping the ladder to steady herself.

She was already wet and ready for his strong fingers. This time he inserted two, steady, rhythmically. She placed one of her feet on the edge of the bed so she could open herself wider to him. His thumb, that fucking amazing thumb, knew exactly how to move against her clit to have her writhing and begging for more.

"Climb up on the bed," he growled.

She shook her head, confused.

He turned her toward the ladder, and she had her first real look at the beds. *A bunk bed? What kind of man rents a hotel room with a bunk bed?*

He gave her ass a playful slap. "Go."

"What are you—?"

He began to kiss her back slowly, caressing every other inch of her while he did. Desire had her climbing the ladder for him without protest or further questioning. Whatever he wanted her up there for, she hoped it felt as good as what he was already doing.

She crawled up onto the top bunk and turned to face him. The side of the bed had one rounded metal railing that was less than two feet wide. "Straddle it," he ordered.

She held onto the top of it and did. The act pulled her legs wide apart, leaving her sex parted and exposed for him. He ran his hands up and down her legs. She could barely breathe she was so excited.

"I want you to come for me," he said with his face parallel to her sex. He leaned forward, darted his hot tongue between her folds, then said, "Do it. Make yourself come for me. Show me how you touch yourself."

At first she thought she wouldn't be able to. She felt too exposed, too vulnerable to do something so private. Their eyes met, though, and he looked at her with a hunger that matched her own, and suddenly instead of feeling vulnerable she felt daring and sexy. She dug her hand into his hair and pulled his face to her sex. "Start me off and I'll finish."

He didn't hesitate. His tongue. His fingers. Together they worked their magic until she was clutching the rail and shaking. She wanted him inside her so badly.

Then he stopped and stepped back. He took his huge, aroused cock in his own hand and said, "Show me."

She bit her bottom lip and half closed her eyes as her hand slid to caress her wet sex. Watching him pleasure himself as she touched herself drove her wilder. Soon, too soon, an orgasm rocked through her.

He made a pained face then ordered her to come to him. She started down the ladder and was about halfway when he placed his hands over hers, halting her descent. "Right there," he whispered.

She heard the rip of a foil package being opened and shivered with anticipation.

"You may have won the condom game; so tell me what you want," he said in a deep, sexy voice.

She glanced over her shoulder at him. "You know what I want."

His lusty smile sent heat rushing through her. "Then, in case I won, tell me."

With him there was no shame, only desire. "I want you to fuck me. Hard. Deep. Kiss my neck. Kiss my back. Don't stop until I cry your name."

He nodded, giving himself over to the passion. One hand went to her hip, the other covered her hand again. He kissed her gently, up and down her back then slid his tip inside her. Slowly in. Slowly out. Then he placed his hand on her lower back and began to pound into her powerfully.

Harder and faster.

Deeper and wilder.

His grip on her hand pinched, but she didn't care. Nothing she'd felt before compared to this. Heat built within her until it ravished her senses. She clung to the ladder, begged him to keep going, and finally sobbed out his name when her second orgasm shook through her.

He continued to pump into her, growled her name in her ear, and with a final thrust also came.

Neither moved at first.

He withdrew and stepped away to clean himself off. She made her way down the rest of the ladder.

A moment later they stood, face to face, both breathing heavily, flushed, sweaty and naked. He smiled first. "One ladder, two beds and a shower. That's only four condoms.

We'll have to find something to do with the rest."

He's joking.

I think.

No, he's serious. Holy mackerel. I don't care if he's the poorest man on the planet. We'll figure something out.

She chuckled. "Admit it, you didn't know about the bunk bed until you saw the room."

He caressed a finger down her cheek, her jaw, her neck and the curve of one breast. "It's the reason I chose the room. Did you like it?"

"Like what?" It was impossible to focus while he lazily traced her areola.

He laughed. "If I had known someone like you existed, I wouldn't have wasted my time with anyone else."

Viviana closed her eyes briefly. She wanted to believe him. Did she dare? When she opened her eyes and looked around, the dorm-like feel of it helped her remain realistic. The room probably had cost fifty dollars. There was no coffee pot, no flat screen TV. It was a bed and a cheap metal woven wire chair. Nothing special. Just the bare minimum.

Which is what we have going as a relationship. The bare minimum. Only because she didn't want to ruin the night by dissecting it, she asked, "What kind of shower does a place like this have?"

"Probably a small one," he said, looking more pleased with that fact than embarrassed. "Want to find out?" He held out his hand in invitation.

She hesitated. *What am I wishing this included? A promise of forever?*

Does forever actually ever happen?

Not in my experience. For now, I'm okay with seeing where this goes.

She took his hand and said, "I would love to."

Chapter Six

LATE THE NEXT morning, Grant woke to his stomach rumbling from hunger. He'd found a flaw in his choice of hotel accommodation and it wasn't the snug sleeping quarters of the bottom bunk. No, that was actually quite pleasant. He wasn't one who normally encouraged women to spend the night because it led to them thinking it meant more than it did.

Waking up with Viviana naked and draped across his chest, however, was something he could get used to. After a marathon of sex that concluded with both of them too sated and too tired to even talk, he was relaxed and didn't want to move.

His stomach growled again.

What kind of hotel doesn't have room service?

He checked his watch. It was almost noon. *I could ask my assistant to deliver food and coffee.*

Bad idea. And I'd still have to get up.

He looked down at Viviana and saw her eyes had opened. He kissed her lips softly. "Good morning."

"Morning," she said grumpily. "I'm sorry, I'm not human before coffee."

He kissed her forehead. "After last night I could forgive you almost anything."

She blushed and brought a hand up to his temple. "You have a bruise. Does it hurt? I felt so bad when you hit your head on the railing."

He winced at her touch but more for sympathy than from pain. The move worked. She shifted upward with concern, her bare breasts sliding up his chest. "Do you want me to get some ice for it?"

He rolled her over and under him. The urgency of their passion came second now to the simple pleasure of holding her. He wanted to get dressed and head back to his place with her, and he didn't care if she took that as a sign that she could leave a toothbrush beside his. Whatever this was between them, it was too good to continue in cheap hotels and public places.

He wanted to tell her that, but the conversation was a complicated one that might be much better had after his trip to Aruba. *Come home with me so I can leave you for a week? Or two? Or however long it takes me to find Stiles?*

I can't take her with me. If there is any chance at all I'll encounter trouble, she belongs here, uninvolved and safe.

He sighed. "I am going out of town for business."

She searched his face and stiffened beneath him. "When?"

"Tomorrow. I don't know how long I'll be gone."

Her gaze fell to his neck. "Where are you going?"

"I'd rather tell you about it when I return."

"I see."

He moved onto his side and turned her face to his. "I may not be able to call you. It'll depend on the situation. When I get back we—"

She laid her hand across his mouth to stop him from saying more. "Don't say anything more. I'm okay with what we've done. I'm okay with you leaving. Just don't lie to me. That's the only thing that could ruin this."

Grant rolled onto his back and groaned.

Fuck.

WHEN VIVIANA HAD told herself she was willing to ride this out, she hadn't expected it to crash and burn so soon. Grant moved to sit on the edge of the bed with his elbows resting on his knees. He looked like a man deciding between two unsavory options.

She knew the male look all too well. *I caught him in a lie, and he doesn't want to tell me the truth; he's either married or in a committed relationship.*

I shouldn't have halted his exit speech. His way was less awkward. No accusations. No apologies. We could have parted with a kiss and a promise to stay in touch.

Viviana scooted off the bed and started to gather her clothing. When he didn't protest, her heart sank. *If I push him for the truth there's a good chance things will get ugly.*

Already in her jeans, she fastened her bra and pulled her shirt over her head. He took his cue from her and also got dressed. Their eyes met, and she realized that even if he was married she couldn't hate him.

Meeting him opened my eyes to how much different my life could be. Someday I'll find all that passion with a man I love— and that man, whoever he is, will be worth holding out for. I can be sexy, and, in my own way, I'm beautiful. How could I hate a man who helped me discover that?

So maybe I don't ask. I don't push. Maybe my gift to him is that I let him leave with a lie. With an awkward, heavy silence they gathered their things and closed up the room. They made it all the way to the elevator before he spoke.

"I can't imagine that I'll be gone for longer than a week. Two at the most. We'll talk when I come back."

She hitched her purse on her shoulder and forced a smile. "Sounds great."

They rode in the elevator without a word. He hailed a taxi for her. As she was about to step into it, he pulled her to him and gave her a deep, lingering kiss that would have brought tears to her eyes if she were the type to cry. She returned the kiss, but the passion that had fired between them the night before was tempered by their mutual somber mood.

When they broke off the kiss, he said, "Don't look at me that way. This isn't goodbye. I'll be back in a week."

"Of course you will," she said with a small smile. "Have a safe trip." As she closed the taxi door, she closed down her heart. Had she listened to it, she would have jumped back out of the taxi instead of giving the driver the address of her apartment. She would have thrown herself into his arms and demanded the truth—whatever it was.

Another part of her, the part she chose to listen to,

thought this was exactly what she deserved. *The harsh reality is that when you fuck a stranger it's not supposed to lead anywhere.*

Audrey was on the couch doing her toenails when Viviana walked into their apartment. It took one look for Audrey to put her polish away and pat the cushion beside her. "I know we're both adults, but I was worried when you didn't come home last night."

"Sorry," Viviana said as she kicked off her shoes and curled up on the opposite end of the couch. "I should have called. I just wasn't ready to talk about it."

Audrey was quiet for a moment, then she said, "One of the things I love about you is that you've always supported me. When I said I wanted to move away, you didn't try to talk me out of it. No matter where my dreams took me, you never judged. I don't care where you've been or who you were with, but I'm glad you're safe."

Viviana scooted across the couch to give Audrey a long hug before sitting back and rubbing her hands over her face. "There is so much to tell you; I don't even know where to begin. Do you remember that jogger yesterday?"

"The one you tripped then had a drink at a juice bar with?"

"We had more than a drink there." Viviana took a deep breath and told her friend everything. She didn't hold back because—hell, this was Audrey. The two of them had researched tampons versus pads when they were teenagers. There was nothing she couldn't tell her. Viviana wrapped the story up with what had gone through her head that morning as she'd left him.

Audrey nodded and said, "It sounds like it wasn't all bad, but I'm sorry it ended the way it did."

"I'm okay with it," Viviana lied, then added, "I will be. I'm not one hundred percent sure it's over, but I'm trying to be realistic."

"What did you say his name was?"

"Grant. Grant Enynaim."

"Honey, I don't want to be the voice of doom, but your instincts are right about this one. Enynaim? Any name? That's a red flag right there. Hey, if the sex was good, does it matter? Men lie. As long as you used protection you can chalk this up to a learning experience."

He lied about his name, too. Was anything he said true? Viviana looked away and Audrey slapped her thigh. "Tell me you used protection."

Viviana grimaced. "Every time but the first."

Audrey rolled her eyes skyward. "Which do you need a refresher lecture on? The birds and bees or STDs?"

"Neither," Viviana shook her head. "It's over, Audrey, and I'm fine."

Audrey picked up her nail polish again and started to apply a second coat to her toenails. "I know I suggested you put yourself out there, but it's time to reel yourself back in. You have to be careful. This isn't Cairo, New York. You're lucky you didn't get hurt."

Viviana nodded even though that wasn't entirely true. She hugged her legs to her chest and tried to block out the images of Grant that kept popping into her thoughts. His laugh. His kiss. The feel of him inside her. The butterflies that filled her chest whenever he looked at her.

To know that none of it was real and that it truly was over did hurt.

No matter what she told herself—the truth was, it hurt like hell.

Chapter Seven

A WEEK LATER Grant walked down the steps of his jet and onto a private airfield outside of Trinity, Canada. Although the small harbor town boasted two hundred permanent residents, there was only one he was interested in meeting. If the mother of the pilot Stiles had paid to lie on his flight log was right, this was where her son had spent one uneventful evening before flying back to Aruba.

The first few days in Aruba had been frustrating. Just as Marc had warned, when Grant had first starting asking questions no one had been willing to discuss Stiles. What he'd found most curious was the fear he saw in some people's eyes at the mere mention of his name.

Grant met with the private investigator Lance had hired and learned nothing more than he already knew. After a couple of days of making no progress, Grant had decided to become more creative.

To get people to open up to him, he fabricated a story about working for the insurance company that covered Stiles's home and clinic. He flashed his fake IDs and said he was trying to earn a commission by proving Stiles had set his own home on fire.

Each time he told that story he learned something new about Stiles. In Aruba, Helene's uncle was loved as well as feared. No one was willing to say a bad word about him, but they did describe how much of his own money he'd poured in, providing health services for those who couldn't afford it.

Grant's break came when he tracked down Stiles's butler. The man had worked for him for a decade and was still angry he'd been let go with no warning or severance pay. Grant offered him five hundred dollars in exchange for any information regarding where Stiles might have gone.

When the man hesitated, Grant had used his cover story and said five hundred dollars was all he had, but if he proved Stiles was guilty, he'd get a bonus from his company and could send him more.

For a man who'd never been good at lying, he found he was better at it than he wanted to be. He layered on a story of two children in college and all the bills that went with it. That had resonated with Stiles's ex-bulter, and he'd told Grant that although he didn't know where Stiles was, he knew the mother of the pilot he'd used to leave the island.

More lies and another small bribe had gained him an address in Trinity, Canada. As soon as he had that, he sent Marc Stone ahead to make sure Stiles wouldn't get far if he ran.

Grant slid into the black SUV he'd hired to take him to Stiles. If he were there for any other reason, he would have taken the time to appreciate the 18th century charm of the small roads, saltbox houses, and churches set against the deep blue of the cold northern ocean. He struggled to keep his thoughts focused on his reason for being there because when his mind wandered it filled with memories of a woman he'd almost called about a hundred times since leaving Boston.

He hated how he'd left things with Viviana. Their final kiss had felt like a goodbye. At the time he'd told himself the truth could wait. She could wait until he came back to hear his reasons for lying to her.

As the week went on, though, he'd thought more and more about how hurt she'd looked when he'd told her he might not be able to call her for a while. *She thought I was brushing her off.*

He could have called her, but he didn't want to keep up the lie. He also didn't feel it was a conversation they should have over the phone.

Just a few more days.

I'll get the answers my family needs then track down Viviana and explain as much of this as I can.

Full disclosure might be worse than saying nothing.

I ditched you the morning after we had phenomenal sex because I had to find out how and why my soon to be sister-in-law's uncle killed my infant brother. Yeah, my family's fucked up.

The SUV parked in front of a blue and white house near the center of town. There was nothing about it that stood out from any of the other houses. Grant scanned the area and saw a man leaning against a tree a few hundred feet down the street. *Marc.*

Grant flicked his head in question toward the house.

Marc nodded.

Grant made a tactical hand motion for Marc to come and then a square to represent the back door and waved him in that direction. In a practiced, smooth move Grant slid his gun from the holster beneath his suit and kept it close enough to his thigh that it would blend in with the dark gray from a distance.

He was going into the situation armed because in his opinion cowards were as unpredictable and dangerous as little dogs. Both panicked and might attack without warning.

He knocked on the front door and stood slightly off to the side so he was not visible through the glass pane in the door. Stiles opened the door, looked around, and tried to slam the door shut as soon as he saw Grant.

Grant shoved his foot in the door to stop it from closing then shoved it back open with his shoulder. He slammed the door closed behind him and raised his gun. "Clarence Stiles, I'm going to give you a chance to make things right by telling me the truth about what happened to my brother, Kent Barrington."

On closer inspection there was little about Clarence Stiles that warranted a drawn weapon. He was thin, almost frail looking, with gray hair and tired eyes. "You must be Asher. I know you by reputation"

"I am not," Grant said impatiently.

Stiles relaxed somewhat. "Are you Ian? The ambassador. Have you come to offer me asylum?"

"No."

The older man scratched his chin. "You're too old to be

the architect, Lance."

"I'm Grant."

"The financial wizard? Why would they send you?"

His temper rose and he holstered his gun. If need be, he could handle Stiles with his bare hands. "Because I'm the one who can best afford to cover up your death if you don't tell me what I want to know."

Stiles went white and swallowed visibly. "How is Helene?"

"She's safe, no thanks to you."

"I knew Andrew would get her out of there. I wasn't as sure I'd be able to do the same. If you see her, tell her I'm sorry I left the way I did. My nerves are shot. Mind if I get a drink?"

Grant shook his head. Stiles looked like he might pass out if he didn't, and that would be counterproductive. Still, he had no sympathy for him. Stiles had entrusted his niece's safety to Andrew, a man he'd just met, then covered his ass by destroying old medical records and fleeing. He was weak in the most disgusting sense. "I have men outside who will shoot if you try to run."

Stiles made his way over to a cabinet, poured himself a shot of whiskey, and downed it in one gulp before pouring himself another. "I'm not afraid to die. I haven't slept through the night in months. I've lost my family, my clinic—everything I spent my life working for. All gone. And I deserved to lose it all. So, please, kill me. You'll be doing me a favor."

"Andrew came home with the impression that you were

responsible for my youngest brother's death."

Stile took another gulp of whiskey. "Responsible yes, but I didn't kill him."

Grant felt some of the tension leave him. It was exactly what he'd assumed. "So it was negligence you covered up."

The liquid in Stiles's glass sloshed as his hand began to shake. "I wish it were."

Grant stepped closer. "How did my brother die?"

"Suffocation," Stiles said weakly. He placed the glass down and moved to sit in a chair, looking as if he might collapse if he didn't. "I didn't know anything about it until after it was done. I would have gone to the police, but it was an officer who told me what had happened. He said I'd be given two choices: a large sum of money to cover up how your brother died or the death of my family. He had photos of my sister, her husband, and Helene. I was scared. A part of me wanted to be heroic like in the movies, but there had already been a death—a nurse. He said anyone who was involved would be erased. I agreed to the cover-up, but I still thought I could do something. Your parents were devastated, but the truth couldn't bring your brother back. I needed to protect my staff. I tried to warn one of them, the one who had delivered your brother, but he said his conscience wouldn't allow him to stay quiet. He died in a car crash soon afterward. They killed him, and it never made the papers. That's when I knew how powerful they were. People could disappear and not make the news."

Grant went to stand above Stiles, shaking his head. "Who would do something so heinous? And why? Why would anyone do that?"

Stiles closed his eyes for a long moment, then said, "A few days later, a man came to see me. He was American. He was the one who arranged for a large sum to be deposited into my bank account. I asked him the same questions. He said the devil is a woman, and her jealousy has no compassion for innocence or age."

With his hands fisting at his sides, Grant growled, "I don't want a riddle. I want a name."

Stiles gripped the arms of his chair. "Patrice Stanfield, your aunt, a woman who, if there is any justice, is rotting in hell—she was the one who paid to have your brother killed. I took her blood money, but I poured it back into the community. One by one, every person who was involved with your brother's birth or death disappeared. Doctors. Nurses. Even the two police officers who had threatened me. I lived every day thinking it would be my last, but they never came for me."

A chill went down Grant's back. He didn't remember ever meeting his aunt Patrice, but she sounded even more demented than her journal had implied. Asher had told him she was the one who had destroyed his father's political career. Had his mother's sister been so sick that she would have gone as far as to have her sister's child killed? Or was this Stiles making up a story to save his own ass? "That doesn't make sense. Why kill just one? Kent was a twin."

Looking sick to his stomach, Stiles said, "I think there was a mix-up. The man who paid me mentioned a baby girl. I think that was who Patrice wanted dead."

"Do you have proof that any of this is true?"

"I destroyed the employee records from that time. No one investigated the murders that followed. I may have had money, but not the kind it would have taken for a cover-up of that magnitude. Only someone very rich, very connected, and very evil could have done this. No, I don't have proof, nor do I have a reason to lie anymore. Look at me. What do you think I have left to lose?"

Grant went over the story, searching for something he could act on. "Are the local police corrupt?"

"I know what they did, but I don't know if they were given the same choices I was. The police chief moved to Argentina. At least, that's what people said."

"Who was the American? Do you know his name?"

"Senator Forn. He retired after that term. He can't help you, though; he killed himself a year later."

"Patrice Stanfield is dead as well. She died a few years ago. Natural causes, they think."

"Thank God she's gone. I probably didn't have to run as I did, but she was the type to set something evil in place, even if there was no longer a need for it. I couldn't risk putting my family in danger again."

"There is no one left to corroborate your story."

"No."

Grant rubbed both hands over his face roughly. Of all the scenarios he'd thought he might uncover, this was by far worse. He'd told Ian he would tell his mother any truth, regardless of how ugly. How could he tell her this?

"Why did you have Helene visit you at all if you were

worried about her safety?"

"I didn't perceive danger for her until your brother start-ed asking questions. Then I became afraid he would stir up old trouble."

Grant walked away from Stiles. He needed a moment to think. From across the room, Stiles asked, "What will you do now?"

Grant answered without turning back to face him. "If you weren't Helene's uncle, I would have you prosecuted for what you've done. Or killed. Or whatever I deemed the least painful for my family. My brother was murdered at your clinic, and you did nothing to honor his memory or bring comfort to his family."

"Is there any comfort to be found in knowing that one's own sister killed one's child?"

"No, there is not."

"I know it's too little too late, but I am so very sorry about what happened to your brother and what it put your family through. I may not have killed him, but Kent's blood is on my hands. I am responsible. You're right—it was my clinic, and the choices I made back then have been my own ticket to hell."

Grant turned then. "I have all I need for now. There will be someone in town who will make sure you can't run again in case I have further questions."

"Will you tell Helene you saw me?"

"I don't know," Grant said with a disgusted shake of his head. "I don't know."

He stepped through the door of Stiles's home and took a

deep gulp of fresh air. He sat down on the top step of Stiles's steps and continued to take deep, calming breaths.

"Did you get what you came for?" Marc asked as he approached.

"No," Grant said in a hollow voice. *I wanted it to be something we could all forgive. A mistake covered up. I didn't want this.*

Until he'd spoken to Stiles, a part of Grant had felt powerful and in control. He was neither. There was no good way to spin what he'd learned. Rather than uncovering something that would bring his mother closure and peace, he now had to decide if some questions should remain unanswered.

I'm sorry, Mom. I didn't find what you need.

And I don't know what to do with the truth.

VIVIANA PEED ON a fourth stick because the positive result on the first three pregnancy testers had to be a mistake. *Because I can't be pregnant.*

I'm too smart to get knocked up by a Mr. Any Name.

Double lines again.

Shit.

So much for trying to forget him.

Two weeks without hearing from the man whose name was now banned in her apartment. Week one had been the hardest. Even after her talk with Audrey, Viviana had clung to a sliver of hope that he would call. She considered herself a good judge of character. Yes, there had been glimpses of arrogance, but overall he'd been decent.

Now I have to face it. His wife was probably away on a

trip, and he was looking for a diversion. I just happened to throw myself at him at the right time.

And the cherry on top? I'm pregnant.

I should have known there'd be a price to pay for cutting loose. Some people live on the wild side and somehow nothing bad happens to them. I stick my toe in a puddle of decadence and now I'm going to be a mother.

Mom, where did you meet my father?

Um, next question please.

Did you love him?

Love? That's hard to feel when you never knew his real last name.

Viviana tossed the testers in the trash and washed her hands before exiting the bathroom. Audrey was stepping out of her shoes near the coat rack but froze when she saw Viviana's face.

"Did someone die?"

"No," Viviana said in a tight voice. "Can we talk?"

"Sure."

They each sat on their usual ends of the small couch. "I'm pregnant."

Audrey's eyes rounded and she blinked a few times. "How sure are you?"

"Four testers sure."

Andrey moved closer and put a hand on Viviana's arm. "What are you going to do?"

"Do?"

"You have choices."

"Like an abortion?"

"Or adoption."

Viviana sat back and put her hand on her still flat stomach. "I'm only two weeks along. I've heard people don't even tell anyone at this stage because it doesn't always stick."

With a sympathetic squeeze of her hand, Audrey said, "Hoping it goes away is not a plan."

"I'm not hoping—" Viviana stopped. Really, she was still in shock. It didn't feel real yet. She thought about what her father had once said about her own existence and knew what she couldn't do. "I couldn't abort a baby or give one away. I'm not judging anyone who could. I just think that every life is precious. Mine. This baby's. Everyone's."

Audrey hugged her. "Any baby would be lucky to have you for a mother."

"I guess." Viviana sucked in a shaky breath. "I hope so. I'm still trying to figure out my life. I don't know if I'm able to guide anyone else along."

With a sympathetic smile, Audrey said, "No one is ever ready."

Viviana searched her friend's face. "So, no lecture about how I should have been more careful?"

Audrey shook her head then smiled. "No, but if it's a girl can you name her Audrey? After all, I am partly responsible."

Viviana laughed even though her stomach was still doing flips. "You did tell me to fuck him."

Audrey bent and cupped her hand as if speaking to the baby. "I thought she knew about condoms."

With a groan Viviana said, "I did. My brain just turned off that day." She placed her hand back on her stomach and rolled back onto the couch so she was looking up at the ceiling. "I don't regret it, though. Not even if it changes my life." If she were honest with herself, she'd known before she'd bought the testers. Her body felt different, and it wasn't simply because it had finally experienced good sex. She thought about her mother and wondered if she'd regretted having a third child after she'd been diagnosed with cancer. *You didn't, did you, Mom? I can't either. Little girl or little boy, this child will grow up knowing it is loved exactly as God made it.* A tear ran down her cheek.

"You're going to be okay, Viviana. You're not alone. You have me. And even if you don't want to hear it, you have your dad and your brothers. We all love you."

Viviana raised her head. It was exactly what she needed to hear, and she wrapped her arms around her best friend. "Thank you, Audrey. I'm still trying to absorb this. I'm scared, but I'm not. Does that make sense?"

"You're not sixteen, so, yeah. There's no reason to be afraid. You can do this."

Viviana nodded. "I can." She sat back again. "How long should I wait before I tell my family?"

Audrey made a pained face. "My opinion? Reconnect with them first. They don't understand why you left or why you've avoided them."

"How do you know that?"

Audrey looked away then back. "I check in with your dad once a week. He worries."

Another tear fell. "He doesn't call me."

"He doesn't want to pressure you. All he and your brothers want is for you to be happy. They don't know how they let you down, but they're hoping you forgive them and go home soon. Things aren't the same without you. Their words, not mine."

Viviana wiped away tears that, once they started to flow, just kept pouring out. She took out her phone and said, "There's nothing to forgive. Except maybe on my part. I needed this time away. For me. How do I explain that?"

"You won't have to. I think they'll be happy if you call and say you love them. And maybe, promise to make Dylan shepherd's pie soon. He's mentioned missing it at least three times since you've been here."

Viviana laughed. "It's his favorite."

"I guessed that."

No longer crying, Viviana picked up the phone. "I've missed Cairo. I've loved being here with you, but Boston is too big for me. Maybe it's time I think about going back— but this time getting my own place." An idea came to her and she said, "Since I work for a fertility clinic, do you think they'd believe I did this on purpose? Single women use the service all the time."

"That baby has a father; they may notice that small detail."

"It doesn't. I'm writing Grant off as a sperm donor."

Audrey shook her head. "You can't do that and you know it."

"You think I want—?"

"This isn't about what you want. Once you decide to keep that baby, what you want comes second to what is best for it. Like it or not, that baby has a father, and one day it will ask you about him."

"Grant is probably married. He doesn't want this baby."

"You don't know that."

"What if he's not at all the man I thought he was? What if he's someone awful?"

"You can't use that as an excuse to take the easy way out."

Viviana sighed. "You don't cut me any slack, you know that?"

"I channel my mother when I think you need it," Audrey smiled.

"When is she coming for a visit? I miss her."

"She and Harry are summering in Venice. It's still weird to think of her with a boyfriend, but she's happy."

Viviana looked down at her phone. She had two calls to make—which should she make first?

She scrolled through her contacts and found Grant's number. "Leave a message," his voice said as the call went directly to his voicemail. She almost didn't leave a message, then said abruptly, "It's Viviana, call me when you have a chance." And hung up.

"He'll call," Audrey said.

"Why now? For two weeks you've been convinced he wouldn't."

"You didn't hear your tone. I'd call if I got that message even if I didn't want to see the person again."

Even if I didn't want to see the person again. Audrey's words repeated in Viviana's head. *Is that how he feels toward me?*

How do I tell a man like that that I'm pregnant with his child?

Maybe I don't if he never calls me back.

She scrolled through her contacts again and chose another number. It picked up on the second ring. "Hi, Dad."

"Hi, baby. How are you?"

Viviana blinked back tears. "Good. I miss you. Boston has been fun, but I'm thinking about getting my own place in Cairo and coming back to work for you if there's still an opening."

"There is always an opening for you. You don't need to rent a place; your room is just as you left it."

"I do, Dad. That's part of why I needed to leave to figure it out. I need a space of my own."

"Then we'll find you one." There was chatter in the background and her father said, "I'm not asking her that. Sorry, your brothers are here."

"Tell Dylan yes, I will make it for him when I come back."

Her father laughed. "She knows you too well, and she said yes, now can I finish my conversation?"

Viviana laughed, too. When she'd first started her journey to find herself, she'd thought she needed to leave this part of her life behind. She was beginning to see that she could have both—she could be herself and be with her family. "I love you, Dad."

He cleared his throat. "I love you, too, baby." Then he growled. "I have to go, Viv. Your brothers are laughing at me, and I may have to beat them. When will we see you?"

Viviana smiled because the worst her father had ever done to any of them was yell. "I could come home for the weekend. I want to give my job two weeks' notice."

"You never did tell us what you do out there."

Yeah, and I'm probably going to keep that one to myself. "I'll text you with the info about when I'm coming."

Chapter Eight

GRANT WAS ON his way back to Boston when he saw he had a voicemail from Viviana. Not calling her for two weeks had never been his plan. When he'd first gotten to Aruba he'd told himself he'd call her as soon as he made some progress. After he'd located Stiles, he'd told himself he would call her once he solved the mystery of what had happened to his brother.

If his brother's death had been due to negligence, Grant would be heading to Viviana's straight from the airport. *But there is no good way for this to play out.*

He listened to her voice message several times and had to remind himself that he barely knew her. Was it possible to miss someone when your time with them had been so brief?

She sounded upset, and it tore at him that he was the reason. In his public as well as his private life, he had a solid reputation for being responsible. He wasn't the love 'em and leave 'em type. Just because something didn't morph into a long-term relationship didn't mean it couldn't end on a good note.

He knew he needed to call her back, but his head was

still spinning from what Stiles had told him. He was confused, angry, and deeply saddened by the situation . . . all to a degree that was foreign to him. He strove to remove his emotions from the equation so he could better decide what to do, but it was proving impossible.

Grant was used to being prepared for nearly every outcome. He hadn't prepared for this. He hated feeling out of control.

Everything Stiles said matches the tone of Patrice Standfield's journal. She was jealous of my mother, jealous of her happy marriage. Would that have driven a woman like her to kill, though?

The phone numbers and lists of names in her journal might have been a hit list. Some of the deaths had been attributed to natural causes or accidents, but after what Stiles had said it was pretty obvious what had happened.

A cover-up of that magnitude would have taken not only a significant amount of money but also powerful connections—all of which Patrice would have had. *Can I say with one hundred percent certainty that Stiles's version is true?*

No.

So, do I tell my family what I learned? It might destroy the progress they've made.

I could lie. I've gotten good at it, but the idea of more sickens me.

Viviana, I wish I had met you a year ago.

Or a year from now.

I can't start a relationship in this headspace.

He dropped his phone into the breast pocket of his jacket. *I will call you. Just not yet. Not while this storm rocks my family.*

When this is over, if you're angry, I'll woo your forgiveness with a shower of flowers and gifts.

If you're sad, I'll do whatever it takes to return a smile to your face.

Just not today.

And, unfortunately, not tomorrow either.

A WEEK LATER, Viviana was sipping bottled water instead of her normal afternoon coffee when the woman at the desk next to her fanned her face and said, "Why were there no single men like that in Boston when I was single? I wonder if my husband would consider an annulment."

Stella was one of the few reasons Viviana would miss Boston. She was a constant source of hilarious outbursts. *One more week, I might as well ask.* "Who are you in love with now?"

Stella waved her over. "Look at this video. Seriously, I wouldn't kick any of the Barringtons out of my bed, but most of them are married. Grant isn't, though. Take a close look and you tell me if you wouldn't agree to just about anything with him."

Grant? Must be something about that name because I've already done just about everything with one of those.

There was no way it could be the same one. She took Stella's phone and swayed on her feet when she saw that it was indeed the man she'd spent three weeks trying to forget. The video was a clip from the news. The announcer was speaking, ". . . along with the normally reclusive billionaire Grant Barrington, CEO of Barrington Financial, who also made a substantial donation to the foundation."

"Grant Barrington," Viviana said aloud.

"Gorgeous, right? You're single. You should try to snag a guy like that."

"How do you know he's not married?"

Stella laughed, took her phone back, and smiled down at the video. "I shamelessly stalk them on social media. I can't help it. The Barringtons are kind of a big deal in Boston. I love to live vicariously through them. Can you imagine being that rich?"

"No." Viviana shook her head and returned to her seat on shaky legs. "I wonder what that does to a person."

"Oh, I'm sure they're all stuck-up assholes, but since I'll never meet them I like to imagine they're not. Sometimes I daydream about having them over for a backyard barbeque just to blow my neighbors' minds. I find shit like that funny. People would want to know how and why, and I'd just shrug and say why not."

"Yeah, why not?" *Was that why he chose me? He thought it would be different . . . funny? Of course he did. Why else would he pretend to be broke?*

Oh, my God, tell me I wasn't a joke to him. It was easier imagining him married.

Her hand went protectively to her stomach. *I'm not a joke, nor are you.*

"Are you okay?" Stella asked. "You look a little green."

Viviana grabbed her purse and stood up. "I'm not feeling

well. Could you tell Dave I went home?" *What's he going to do? Fire me?*

"Sure."

Viviana was out on the street in a blink of an eye and in the back of a taxi a moment later.

"Where to?" the driver asked.

Viviana did a quick search on the Internet for Barrington Financial then she read off the address. On the way, she called her best friend. "Audrey, I can't meet you for our run. I not only know his last name, but also where he works."

"Holy shit. Do you want me to come with you?"

Viviana loved her more for asking, but she said, "No, but I need you to give me another one of your mom talks because I'm so angry I might slug him. He's rich, Audrey. Do you know what that means? Everything he said to me was a lie. None of it was real. He's probably been laughing about it since. I bet he thought it was hilarious that I had no idea who he was."

"Calm down, Viv. You don't know that."

"I'm going to confront him, Audrey, but I'll tell you right now that if he is as big of a dick as I think he is, I'm not going to tell him about this baby. I'll give him one chance to sound like a human being and not some egomaniac. That's it. If he's not a good person I'm not letting him near my child. This baby will never feel like it's not good enough. Never."

"You need to calm down, Viv. You can't go to see him like this."

"It didn't work, Audrey. I still want to punch him."

"Should I start looking for bail money?"

"Maybe . . . No. I'm going to be a mother soon. I can't have a record or they'll never let me volunteer in a school. But he needs to see how much he hurt me. He needs to know that the way he treated me wasn't right. I'm not a joke. I'm a person and I don't care if we did have sex before we should have, he should have had the decency to return my call."

"Be careful, Viv."

No, not this time. This time I'm going to say exactly how I feel and let the chips fall as they will.

Chapter Nine

I N HIS OFFICE, Grant leapt to his feet, nearly dropping his cell phone as he did. "What do you mean Asher found Stiles?"

Lance's voice rose, revealing how worried he was. "I mean he tracked him to a town in Canada. I didn't even know he was looking for him. All I know is Emily called me up in a panic this morning because Asher asked Andrew to go on a trip with him but wouldn't tell her to where. The last thing Andrew needs is to have to pick between Asher and Helene's uncle. I don't know what Asher was thinking."

Fuck. This is my fault for stalling on telling them. "Where is Asher now?"

"When I spoke to them they were heading for the airport."

"Shit. Okay, call Ian and tell him we might need him. We either have to stop Asher from going or get to Stiles first."

"I know. I told him not to go, but he wouldn't listen to me. He'll listen to you, Grant. I mean, we all want to find out what Stiles knows, but not like this."

No, not this way. It's time for me to tell them what I know.

"I'll stop Asher, then we need to have a family meeting—without Mom and Dad. Are you free?"

"I can be. Willa will want to be there, too."

Grant almost said that wouldn't be a good idea, but she was family. They would all find out eventually. "Fine. Call Kenzi and Dax, also. I have to go now or I won't catch Asher before he flies off." He hung up before Lance had a chance to respond.

Following his gut, he called Marc Stone. "Marc, I need a specific private plane to immediately discover it has mechanical difficulties. Asher's. He located Stiles. He has Andrew with him. After I hang up with you I'm going to try to reason with him, but in case that fails I want him stuck on the ground."

"I'll see what I can do," Marc said.

"No, make it happen." Grant hung up abruptly again and dialed Asher's number. When Asher didn't pick up, he called Andrew. "Andrew, it's Grant."

"Grant, I'm with Asher. We found Stiles."

"I know. Put him on the phone."

"Why? What's going on?"

"I need to talk to Asher."

"If you know something about Stiles I have every bit, if not more, of a right to know. Helene needs answers as much as we do."

Grant sucked in a deep, calming breath. "Then put me on speakerphone."

"Fine. We can both hear you now."

"We'll fill you in when we get back, Grant, but we found Stiles. Andrew and I are heading up there to get some answers out of him," Asher said in a hardheaded, overconfident tone.

"Are you at the airport yet?"

"We're pulling in now," Andrew answered.

Come on. Come on. Just then a text arrived from Marc confirming landing gear issues had been discovered on Asher's private plane. Plan B was a go. Now back to plan A. "Turn around and come to my office instead. I'm calling an emergency family meeting."

"A what?" Asher barked.

"We need to talk. All of us without Mom and Dad. There is something I need to tell everyone."

"No way. I'm not giving Stiles another chance to run," Asher answered.

"He can't run. I have people making sure he stays put."

"How? We've only known his location for hours," Andrew asked.

"I've known for a week," Grant admitted.

"You knew where Stiles was and didn't tell us?" Grant could picture Asher's face flushing with anger. "What else are you not telling us? Probably not much or you would have said something. He wouldn't talk to you, would he? Well, he'll talk to me."

"Don't go see Stiles until after we talk."

Asher made a frustrated sound. "Sorry, Grant. We're going. If you want we can compare stories when we return."

"Andrew, I want to speak to Asher privately. Could you

take me off speakerphone please?"

Andrew started to say, "I don't see—"

"I know, but do it," Grant interrupted.

"Okay," Andrew said in a tone full of both respect and trust. "Here's Asher."

"Asher?" Grant asked.

"Yes," Asher answered impatiently.

"Wake the fuck up and listen to me. You're scaring the shit out of your wife, and you're about to put Andrew, who we just got back from a dark place, into a very bad situation. You have too much to lose to continue to let your temper control you. You're a father now. Your place is with your wife and son. Andrew's place is with Helene. I said I would handle finding Stiles and I have. Come to my office now, and I'll tell all of you what I know."

A much more humble Asher asked, "Why would Emily be scared?"

Grant sighed. "Because she loves you but also knows you're a hothead with things like this. You have a good woman, Asher, but you'll lose her if you don't start thinking like a team with her."

"Emily knows—"

"She called Lance because she was so upset."

Asher was quiet for a long moment. "I hate that this has hung over our family as long as it has. I just want us to be free of it."

"I feel the same way," Grant said calmly. Unfortunately, things would likely get worse before they got better, especially when everyone heard Stiles's version of Kent's death. "But you need to go home, apologize to your wife, hug her if she'll let you, then come to my office."

"I love Emily. She and Joseph are my life. Nothing is more important to me," Asher said quietly. "Nothing."

"I believe you. Emily does, too. Now prove us right."

"I suppose I should tell my pilot we're not going anywhere."

"He knows," Grant couldn't resist adding.

"What did you say?" Asher asked.

"That plans can change at any moment," Grant added only because revving up Asher more was the last thing he wanted to do. One day, when all of this was a distant memory, he'd tell Asher he wouldn't have made it off the runway.

Or not. There was sometimes an advantage to being underestimated.

After hanging up, Grant plunked himself down at his desk and rested his head in his hands. There were so many ways this meeting could go wrong. He couldn't demonize Stiles because it would hurt Helene. On the other hand, keeping the truth from his family had just proven more potentially destructive than telling them.

Stiles had believed Helene and her parents would be in danger if he hadn't cooperated. He needed to stress that part. Stiles used that as an excuse again regarding why he'd left Helene in Andrew's care. It was a weak excuse at best, but it might lessen the conflict for Andrew.

If all of that somehow went well, they would still need to decide how to tell their mother that her sister had hired someone to kill one of her babies. He was at a loss for how to do that.

Grant's secretary buzzed his office phone. "Whoever it is, Sue, take a message. And clear my schedule for the morning. The only ones I want to see are my family when they arrive."

"It's not a phone call, Mr. Barrington. There's a woman here to see you."

He raised his head and tried to remember who he'd made appointments to see that day. Nothing. His normally flawless memory failed him. "Tell her I'm sorry, but we'll have to reschedule. I'm not seeing clients today."

"She—"

"Not today, Sue."

"I'M SORRY, MISS Sutton, but he isn't seeing anyone today," the secretary said with a polite and somewhat apologetic smile. "If you leave contact information I'll look for an opening in his calendar later this week."

I should have known he wouldn't see me, he didn't even have the balls to answer my phone call. He's probably in there shaking in his shoes, hoping I'll go away.

Well, I'm not going anywhere. Not until I say my piece.

"Later is not good enough."

The secretary's eyebrows furrowed. "I wish there were something I could do, but he asked me to clear his schedule for today. He doesn't sound like he's in a very good mood."

"And that's unusual?" Viviana asked sarcastically. He probably treated her like crap.

"It is. I have worked for Mr. Barrington for six years and

couldn't ask for a better employer. He's fair, he listens, and whenever I've needed—"

"I'm not leaving without speaking to him," Viviana said abruptly. She couldn't stomach listening to someone sing the praises of him while she was still so angry.

"Maybe if I gave him your name?" the secretary suggested tentatively.

Losing patience, Viviana walked past her desk and opened the door herself. "I'll tell him myself."

"Sue, I thought I made myself clear—Viviana!"

At least the bastard still remembers my name. "I wouldn't be here if you returned phone calls."

His secretary rushed in on Viviana's heels. "Mr. Barrington, I'm so sorry. She just—"

"It's fine, Sue. Close the door on your way out."

As soon as the door closed behind Viviana, she marched toward him until she reached his desk, then stopped and planted her hands on her hips. "I don't care how rich you are, it doesn't give you the right to treat people the way you do. I'm not a piece of trash to be tossed aside when you're done like I'm nothing. Regardless of how you feel about me, even if all we were ever going to have was a weekend, you didn't have to end it the way you did."

"You're right."

"Damn straight I'm right. We're both adults. We had sex. And a lot of it. I wasn't expecting a relationship out of it, but I didn't think you'd brush me off as coldly as you did. Or that so much of what you'd told me would turn out to be a lie."

He rubbed his hands over his face like a man suffering from exhaustion and trying to focus. "I was planning to call you and explain."

"Really? What were you going to explain? That you're an arrogant, entitled asshole who doesn't have the balls to have an adult conversation the next day?"

Grant tented his fingers beneath his chin. One side of his mouth twitched, and she stepped closer. If he smiled she really would belt him. "Something along that vein but worded differently."

She jabbed his chest with a finger. "You think this is a joke? Maybe that I'm a joke? I'm not. I might have been the best thing to ever happen to you, but you'll never know that because you're—"

His kiss took her by surprise and sent her senses haywire. His ability to arouse her even when she was imagining strangling him infuriated her but didn't make the kiss any less soul-shattering. When he lifted his head, he held her to him in a tight hug. Her body was literally shaking as it attempted to shift from angry to turned on and back to angry. After a few minutes of weakly savoring the feel of his arms around her, the tickle of his breath on her neck, and the rekindling of a heat that no one else had ever lit in her— she pushed herself out of his arms.

He turned his back to her, and she opened her mouth to tell him off again but the slump of his shoulders confused her. He walked over to the window of his office and stared out over the city. "Sorry. I shouldn't have done that."

Which part, she wanted to demand but there was something heart-wrenching about seeing the cocky, strong man she'd slept with looking like the weight of the world was on his shoulders. *Is it an act?*

Why wouldn't it be? Everything he said was a lie. Maybe this is how a liar of that magnitude looks when he's confronted.

But it felt like more.

She didn't want to, but she cared. She walked over to stand beside him. "Are you okay?"

He glanced at her then shook his head in disgust. "You're too nice. I've been a complete ass to you. You have every right to be angry."

There was something in his tone that pulled at her heart even as she fought against it. "I'm still angry, but that doesn't mean I would celebrate anything bad happening to you. Compassion is something decent people offer one another. It's right up there with honesty and respect."

"Ouch," he said, turning to look at her. "I'm fine. Just family issues. How are you?"

It was a moment of connection, sincerity. At least it felt like it. "Honestly? Hurt and confused. You could have told me you wanted it to be over. You didn't have to promise to call or act like you felt something toward me."

He ran a hand through his hair and rubbed his hand over his eyes again. "I do feel something for you, but I have a lot going on in my life right now. Things I'm not ready to tell anyone—least of all someone I just—"

Screwed for a weekend? Viviana sucked in a breath audibly. "Please stop. I have one last question then I'll go. And if you're rich why act like you're not? Why take me to a cheap hotel? Was it some kind of sick game to you? If so, it wasn't a kind one."

His expression tightened to one of pain, then he said, "In full disclosure, I found pretending to be poor exciting. It had come to my attention that I was out of touch with regular people. I went jogging by the river that night to meet some. Then I met you. You were just the kind of average, ordinary person I was looking for."

Average. Ordinary. Fuck you. Anger rose in her again, pushing back both her attraction and her sympathy for him. "There's a term for that. It's called slumming."

"That makes it sound—"

Viviana took a step back. "Of course, you probably have a much more polite word for rich people fucking regular people for fun. How crass of me."

"That's not what I mean," he said, taking a step toward her.

"Stop lying. God, have the balls to be honest about what you did. That's all I want. I picked you out of a crowd because I wanted to sleep with a stranger to make myself feel better. You wanted to taste *average*. Look me in the eye and just say it."

"I did. I wanted to see what it would be like, but then—"

She covered her ears. "I don't want or need the lies." She lowered her hands. "I'm sorry I barged into your workplace, but I needed answers and now I have them." With that she turned and strode toward the door.

"Viviana," he called out.

Before she had time to turn, the door opened and Sue

stuck her head in. "Your brother, Lance, is here, Mr. Barrington, along with his wife, Willa. Should I have them wait?"

"No need," Viviana growled. "We're done."

She heard Grant call out after her again, but she bolted through his secretary's office, past people she didn't spare a glance at, and to the stairs. The way she felt required immediate escape, no time for an elevator.

Chapter Ten

GRANT CHASED HER as far as the outer hallway, but when she chose the stairs rather than chance him catching up with her, he let her go. Had he really wanted to, he could have grabbed her arm before she made it out of his office, but he'd been disgusted with himself when he'd seen their time together through her eyes. Disgusted enough to wonder if she was right.

What kind of man treats a woman the way he treated her?

Standing in the hallway outside his secretary's office, Grant came close to retching. *I should have told her that average was a hell of a lot better than whatever I am.*

I should have said something to ease her pain.

She is ordinary in the most extraordinary way. Grounded. Honest. Strong. All the qualities that make what she said about how she could have been the best thing to ever happen to me absolutely true.

I did all of it wrong, but I want a second chance to get it right.

I should have told her that.

Our time together was a game of sorts, but one that woke me up to what my life is missing.

Why didn't I say that? That's the truth she should have heard.

Maybe, then, she wouldn't have left.

He looked over his shoulder at his brother and sister-in-law waiting for him. The ding of the elevator announced its arrival and when the door opened more of his family poured out. He laughed even though he found no humor in the moment. *Even if I had found the words to convince her to stay, what would I have done? Invited her to this shitfest?*

Don't close your heart too firmly, Viviana Sutton. As soon as I sort this out, I'm coming for you.

"Who was that?" Lance asked from the doorway.

"Who was who?" Kenzi asked as she joined them with her husband, Dax, at her side.

"I didn't see anyone," Dax supplied.

Ian stepped out of another elevator. "Did I miss something? I came over as quick as I could."

Helene arrived a moment later. "Hi. Is Andrew here yet? He called and said he and Asher were picking up Emily first, but he wouldn't tell me what this is about."

Before Grant had a chance to answer Helene, Ian asked, "Did you find out something?"

"My uncle? Did you find my uncle?" Helene's voice trembled.

Grant took a deep breath and raised his hands. "Let's all go into the conference room so we can sit and talk. I don't want to say anything until everyone is here."

As they followed him into the conference room, Kenzi said, "It can't be good or you'd have Mom and Dad here."

"It's not good, and it's not rock-solid provable, but it is something you all need to hear and help me decide what to do next with the information."

There were several long somber moments in which his siblings moved closer to their partners. The air was heavy with dark anticipation.

When Asher, Emily, and Andrew arrived, Grant closed the door and told everyone to sit. To his surprise even Asher took a seat next to Emily, looking more shaken than Grant had ever seen him. If Grant had to guess, Emily had told him what he needed to hear. She didn't look much happier than he did, but they were holding hands and that was hopefully a good sign.

Grant cleared his throat. "I found Clarence Stiles a week ago. He's in Trinity, Canada." For Helene's benefit, he added, "He's safe and apologetic."

Helene nodded and Andrew put his arm around her shoulder. The grateful look he gave Grant had Grant clearing his throat again. "After my trip to Aruba, I expected him to confirm that Kent's death had been the result of gross negligence which had sparked a deadly cover-up. Unfortunately, the facts he provided me paint a much uglier picture of what happened."

"What did he say?" Helene asked quietly.

"There are more victims in his version than heroes. I can't confirm everything he said, but it does correlate well with our aunt's journal."

Collectively, the group seemed to hold their breath.

Grant continued, "The way Stiles tells it, Mom's sister hired someone to kill one of her babies."

"What does that mean? One of?" Ian demanded.

"Stiles believes Kenzi was the target, but Kent was killed instead. Stiles only became involved after the murder when he was shown photos of Helene and her parents, and he was threatened with their deaths if he didn't help in the cover-up."

Kenzi gasped and huddled closer to her husband, who was taking it all in with deadly calm. "Why would anyone want to kill me?"

Grant looked around the room wishing he could spare his family from this. "I have read and reread Patrice's journal. I believe she was a sociopath who was jealous of the life our mother made for herself. Mom was happy. Patrice wanted to destroy that. She genuinely hated Mom and us by default. It could have been as simple as not wanting Mom to have a girl or twins. I don't know."

His family asked all the same questions he'd asked Stiles. They wanted someone to pay for what had happened, but everyone involved was gone. Except Stiles.

It was a painful, enormous elephant in the room.

Helene's eyes were brimming with tears. Andrew looked like his heart was breaking along with hers.

Kenzi was half scared, half in shock. Dax was coiled like a cobra in the grass.

Lance and Willa were sad and at a loss for what to say.

Ian was processing.

And Asher—his attention was where it belonged, on his wife and how she was handling the news.

Flexing his shoulders, Grant took on the first hurdle his family faced. "I wanted to hate Stiles, but I don't know what I would do if I thought someone would hurt any of you. I'd like to think I'd make better choices. Everyone wants to be a hero, but sometimes life doesn't offer that option. The fact is a lot of people lost their lives over this. He took money, yes, but would Helene be with us today if he hadn't? None of us know the answer to that. So, was he wrong? Yes. But can we let God be the one who punishes him? I think we have to or we continue to breathe life into the evil Patrice brought to our family."

Helene started to cry against Andrew, and Grant waited for his siblings to respond. Asher shared a look with Emily then leaned across the table and offered his hand to Helene.

Helene placed her hand in his. Andrew covered both with his. One by one, wordlessly, each of his siblings and spouses added their hand to the pile. Then Grant added his to the top and said, "This is what matters: family."

The group slowly relaxed back into their seats and Ian slapped his hand down on the table. "So, what do we tell Mom?"

VIVIANA DIDN'T CRY on the way back to her apartment. She refused to. For the sake of her baby, she was determined to remember Grant as a sperm donor. Working for a fertility clinic had introduced her to plenty of women who didn't think a male presence was a necessary part of a family unit.

None of them hated their donors. In fact, they were often grateful there was a system in place that allowed them to be independent mothers. She wasn't going to remember Grant as an elitist asshole, she would remember him as male, late thirties, tall, brown hair, brown eyes, probably college educated, health history unknown.

She didn't cry when she called Audrey to tell her that meeting Grant Barrington had been a disappointing experience. Anger and confusion nipped at her, but she shoved both back as she calmly informed Audrey she'd decided not to tell Grant about the baby.

This time Audrey didn't argue.

She also told her she was moving home earlier than expected. Her job had told her two weeks wasn't necessary so she wasn't concerned with that. She did hate leaving Audrey so quickly, but she offered to pay for an extra month's rent. Audrey wouldn't hear of it.

"When will you go?" she asked.

"I don't know yet. I need to talk to my dad before I make any big decisions. Either way, it's not like I could stay here."

Always quick-witted, Audrey had joked, "You could, you'd just start paying two thirds of the rent."

Had Audrey been in the room, Viviana would have hugged her then. Some friendships were fragile and dissolved when schedules or circumstances changed. Audrey had become family. "Unless I have twins."

"Oh, Lord." Audrey laughed. "You haven't been sipping that fertility cocktail have you? Are you having a litter?"

Viviana laughed along, and it felt good. "I'd give you the runt."

"You would."

"Yes, I would."

"I was going to work late tonight, but tell me if you need me."

"No, I have this. No matter what I decide, I still have to pack."

"True. Okay. Call me when you know something."

"I will."

Viviana wandered from room to room in the apartment, gathering her courage and the right words. She wasn't a child anymore. It wasn't like her father could ground her.

She just didn't want him to be disappointed in her—or her child.

She dialed his number and took a seat at the kitchen table because that's where she and her father'd had most of their serious talks when she was younger. "Hi, Dad."

"Hi, baby, what's up?"

"I'm pregnant, Dad."

"Oh, okay." She recognized his shocked, stalling phrase.

"I'm really early on, so I wasn't going to say anything yet, but it's something that has to be considered when I think about moving home."

Her father cleared his throat. "What about the father?"

She could have lied then, but she wanted a better relationship with her father and that required honesty. "It was nothing serious." Even though she told herself she was okay with it, saying the words still hurt. She reminded herself harshly that she hadn't known him long. Whatever feelings she might think she had for him were likely side effects from all the hormones rushing around her body. *I refuse to miss a man I never really knew. Yes, meeting him changed my life in more ways than I was prepared for, but I will not be sad if it ends up meaning nothing to him.*

"Is he going to be part of the child's life?"

"No."

"I'm sorry."

"It's okay, Dad. There's something I need to ask you, though, before I come back."

"Anything."

Viviana let out a slow breath before saying, "Were you ever scared?"

"About parenting?" He made a pained sound. "Of course I was. And it doesn't get easier. You always worry if you're doing it right." He was quiet a moment, then added, "When your mother died, I looked into sending you to live with your aunt. I spend all my time with men. I thought you might be better with someone who knew about female things. In the end, I loved you too much to let you go, and I had to hope that was enough."

Viviana did cry then. Silent tears because her father didn't need to know what she'd had in her head and heart for too long. "You did a great job, Dad. That's why I want to raise my baby around you, Dylan, and Connor. I want this baby, and I want it to be around people I know will love it."

"Then you're right to come home, baby. Does this mean you want your old room?"

Her time in Boston had helped her find her voice and understand that it was okay to want a place of her own. "No, I still want my own place, but maybe close enough that we could walk over."

Her father laughed. "Do you remember Henry and Stella Hahn? They're selling their house. It's three blocks away, which might be good exercise for you when you get fat."

"You did not just say that."

"I did." He laughed again and a huge smile spread across her face. The one thing construction company owning dads didn't do was sugar things up.

"Well, Grandpa, three blocks sounds like a long way for someone who will soon have a walker, but we'll meet you halfway—me, the baby, and my big post pregnancy butt."

"Hang on, your brothers just came in. Hey, Connor and Dylan, start washing your hands more, Viviana is having a baby." He groaned. "No, not right this minute. She hasn't been gone that long. I worry about them, Viv. I really do. We have to find them wives or something. I won't always be around to explain life to them."

"You're not going anywhere for a long, long time, Dad."

"No, I'm not, baby," her father assured her quickly.

Viviana hadn't meant her comment to sound as dramatic as it came out. She couldn't imagine her life without him. Milestones in her future flashed before her eyes and she wanted him at all of them. He needed to be the one to teach her child to fish. Boy or girl, she wanted her child to enjoy the side of her father she had enjoyed. Suddenly all those memories of sharing bagged lunches on construction sites with her family and their crew, listening to questionably appropriate stories from how they'd all spent their weekend, wasn't so bad. She wanted her child to know the joy of learning to ride a bike on the shaded sidewalk of the tree-lined street she grew up on. Odd how her view of so much had changed since she'd been away. *I guess sometimes you can't see how good something is until you experience life without it.*

What would Grant think of that kind of life? Would he consider his privileged childhood better? If she'd told him about their baby would he have tried to take the child from her, wrongly thinking he could give it a better life? The mere idea of that sent a shiver down her back. *It doesn't matter what he would or wouldn't think since he'll never know about this child.*

Chapter Eleven

TWO PAINFULLY LONG days later, Grant ended his day by changing into jogging clothes and heading out the front door of his building. He needed to clear his head before he saw his family that night. His siblings had debated when and what to say to their parents and decided to wait until their mother's latest charity event was over. Kenzi organized a mid-week family dinner under the guise of Andrew wanting to see everyone again before heading back to Florida where he and his wife now had a beautiful house near her parents' animal rescue.

After this, the worst of it would be over. If their mother took the news hard, that was to be expected, but she wasn't alone. Together they would help her through it. His family finally had the truth. Now they could let go and heal.

He checked his watch and was about to take off in a run when he heard a man say, "That's him."

"Are you sure? He doesn't look rich."

The hair on the back of Grant's neck went up. *Was I too confident there would be no consequence to learning the truth? I'm smarter than this. I should have taken into account that there might be someone left who would be afraid of loose ends.*

He turned slowly on his heel, his body coiled and readying to dodge a bullet if need be. Two tall blond men in jeans and plaid shirts didn't look like hitmen, but since he didn't have much experience with those he really couldn't say.

"I've seen a photo of him. That's definitely him," one of the men said.

"You think he can hear us?"

They each were about Grant's height and build, but they weren't exactly intellectually intimidating. Grant relaxed somewhat. "Who are you looking for?"

One of the men stepped forward and scowled at him. "Are you Grant Barrington?"

"If I am?" Grant asked, still assessing both threat and angles for defense.

"We're here about Viviana Sutton."

He grabbed the nearest one by the front of his shirt and hauled him closer. If these buffoons thought they could threaten him by threatening her, they were about to be introduced to reality. "If anything happens to her, there is nowhere you or anyone you care about could hide. I'm not Stiles. I'll strike first, and I'll keep striking until you and yours are erased."

"No wonder she didn't tell him. Dylan, I told you coming here was a bad idea."

"Stop being such a pussy, Connor. How are we going to scare him if you piss yourself? It doesn't matter who he is. We're not leaving until we know he won't show his face in Cairo."

Dylan? Connor? They couldn't be. Grant released the front of the man's shirt. "First of all, I can hear you. Second, is your last name Sutton?"

Connor said, "He probably wants it for the police report."

Dylan added, "We didn't do anything wrong. He threatened us. Dad couldn't be mad at that. He grabbed you. We're still fine."

"Dad told us to stay out of it. Now he knows our names. Viviana is going to kill us if she finds out we did this."

So, this is Viviana's family. They could not have been more different than Grant's brothers. *I kind of like them.* "Why are you here? Is Viviana okay?" *I knew I hurt her, but enough that she went home?* That thought made him sick.

"Maybe she was right not to tell him. Listen to him. Does he sound like someone you'd want to share custody of a child with?" Connor asked.

Dylan grabbed his brother's arm and yanked him away for a private conference a few feet away on the sidewalk. Connor's question ricocheted through Grant.

Without hesitation Grant joined their think tank. *No. She can't be pregnant.* Then he remembered how they hadn't used protection the first time. "Is Viviana pregnant?"

"We are so screwed," Connor said, shaking his head.

Dylan turned and went nose to nose with Grant. "I don't care who you are or what you think you could do. If you mess with Viviana again, we have large machinery and huge fields. That's the kind of erasing that would meet you in Cairo."

"Is she pregnant?" Grant repeated his question in a harsher voice.

"We might as well tell him. He knows now," Connor said.

Dylan nodded. "Okay. I'll give him his answer." With no warning, he pulled back and nailed Grant, fist to his jaw, with enough force that Grant stumbled back a few steps. "Now we go home," Dylan said as he turned away.

Before Connor followed suit he said, "You took advantage of one of the sweetest, kindest women in the world. Maybe you're not scared of us now, but try to see her again and you will be."

Grant stood on the sidewalk for a moment, rubbing his bruised jaw as the ramifications of what he'd just learned sunk in. *Viviana is pregnant with my child. Pregnant.*

I'm going to be a father.

Holy, shit. I'm going to be a father.

Marc Stone appeared beside him. "You okay?"

Grant turned slowly to face him and mocked, "I'm your silent shadow. If you see me, I'm not doing my job right, but I'm always there. Where the fuck were you a second ago?"

Looking unfazed by the question, Marc shrugged and said, "For international criminals, Mafia, hired hitmen—I've got your back. You knock up someone's little sister and her family comes for you—you take that shit like a man."

Grant laughed even though there was not too much he found funny about the situation. "I'm going to be a father."

"It does look that way."

His phone beeped with incoming messages from his family asking him not to be late to dinner. He'd never been late . . . ever, so their texts were more about their own level of anxiety than actual reminders. *I just have to get through tonight then I'll call Viviana.*

Or go see her.

He made a pained face. *That should be interesting.* He turned to Marc and took a stab at a joke. "This is all your fault, you know. You're the one who told me I needed to get out there in the world and learn how regular people behaved."

Marc smiled and shook his head. "You certainly did that. Not that you asked my opinion, but yes, I do think they hate you."

"That's going to prove awkward because I want to be with Viviana. I was waiting for the situation with my family to settle before I sought her out again, and this hasn't changed how I feel. In fact, it gave me more of a reason to try again with her."

Marc groaned. "You're not going to say it like that to her, are you?"

Grant paused because he didn't yet have a better plan. "Of course not."

"Don't they teach you anything about women in billionaire school?"

"Not women like Viviana. I've never met anyone like her. She's smart, she's beautiful. She's strong. She doesn't care about my money. I couldn't have chosen a better mother for my child."

"Your challenge will be convincing her this isn't all about

the baby."

"It's not. I was already planning to convince her to give me a second chance."

"Yeah. Crash course on regular women 101: she's not going to believe that."

Grant rubbed his sore jaw again. "You don't know me very well if you think I'm intimidated by a challenge. Tell me something is impossible, and I will prove you wrong every time. You should understand that. As Andrew would say: Adapt. Improvise. Overcome. That's exactly what I'm going to do."

"I have to give you props for confidence."

"I do have one question, though."

"Okay. Shoot."

"Do you think I need to buy plaid shirts?" He shuddered at the thought.

A FEW HOURS later, Grant, along with his siblings and their significant others, stood in the living room of his parents' home waiting for their mother's reaction to the news that her sister was responsible for Kent's death. The room remained painfully silent as Sophie took hold of her husband's hand while sinking into a chair, her face losing all color as she did.

"How certain are you that this is true?" she asked.

Grant went to her side and sank to his haunches so his face was level with hers. "All we have is Stiles's word, but it seems to be supported by your sister's journal."

His mother covered her eyes with shaking hands. "I tried to reconcile with Patrice so many times, but she was so angry. Always so angry. I told myself if I kept including her, one day I would reach her. I couldn't give up hope on her. That's why I called her from Aruba to tell her I was going into labor early. I gave her all the information about where we were. And she took my baby." Tears filled her eyes. "This is my fault."

Dale sunk to his knees and took her hands in his. "No. Your sister was a sick, sick woman, but we don't have proof that she went this far."

With tears running freely down her cheeks, she said, "You don't have to protect me anymore, Dale. My sister was jealous when I first told her I was expecting twins and that one was a little girl. You warned me to cut Patrice out of my life. You said she was getting worse rather than better, but I didn't listen. I loved her; we were close as children. All I wanted was to have that back. I should have protected our children from her. I should have protected you. She ended your career by spreading those rumors, and I was so afraid of losing her I asked you not to retaliate. How do you not hate me?" She looked around at her children. "How do you all not hate me?"

Asher placed a hand on Sophie's shoulder. "How could we? You're the one who showed us how to love. It's not always easy, and it involves a lot of forgiveness, but you showed us how to be a family." He turned to his wife who came over to hold his other hand. "No matter what your sister did, she didn't break us."

Lance walked over hand in hand with Willa. "Look around, Mom. We're all here because we love you, and there is nothing anyone could ever do that would change that."

Ian stepped closer and stood beside his father. "You, too, Dad. None of us knew the reason you made the choices you did, and we judged you harshly for it, but this is our chance to move forward with open eyes."

Their dad nodded, tears filling his eyes. "All we can do is make loving decisions and hope they're right. Only time reveals which were mistakes, but you can live with them if you have good in your heart. I was wrong so many times, but I love all of you more than you'll ever know."

"We know, Dad," Grant said kindly.

In the silence that followed, Grant realized Andrew and Helene were hanging back. He met Andrew's gaze across the room. "We are not the sum of what has been done to us, nor should we carry the guilt of the wrong others have done. We have our answers now. It's time to move on and heal."

Andrew hugged Helene and nodded. As much as Grant wanted this meeting to be over, he wanted Andrew to get what he needed from it. Patrice would not take a second brother from him.

"No," Sophie said in a soft voice before repeating the word with more force. "No. I can't move on yet. I know Kent isn't dead."

Grant's heart broke for his mother. It would take time for her to fully absorb what she'd heard that day. "He is dead, Mom. We buried him, remember? Now we've learned how he died."

His mother surged to her feet, grabbed Grant's forearm, and looked around to each member of her family as she spoke. "No one believed me when I said I'd held Kent. I thought I'd gone crazy because I knew I had held him. I knew it. Just like I know he's alive now. He's out there somewhere. We have to find him."

Asher said, "Tell us what you need us to do, Mom, and we'll do it. You deserve to have answers."

Shaking his head, Ian said, "There are no more answers to find. We know where Kent is."

Sophie's grip on Grant's arm tightened. "Grant, you believe me, don't you? Kent is alive."

"I'm sorry, Mom," Grant said gently.

With her husband in tow, Kenzi stepped forward and said, "I've always known Kent is out there. I would know if he's dead. He's not."

Sophie rushed over to Kenzi and wrapped her arms around her. "What we feel can't be wrong. As his twin, you have a closer bond to him than anyone else. If you believe me, I know I'm right. A mother knows when her child is alive." She raised her chin. "We need to exhume the body we buried. It's not Kent."

Ian jumped on that. "There's no way to do that quietly. If that gets in the news—"

A rabbit hole that could only lead to pain opened before Grant. He'd thought the truth would bring his mother comfort, but it hadn't. However much he wanted to deny it, Ian's instincts were correct. Once his family started on this path the news would run with it.

Not only would their family tragedy once again become public interest, but wherever it led would be, too. There would be no way to protect Helene from the possible backlash. And, for what? To discover an even more revolting truth? Patrice had hired someone to kill either Kenzi or Kent. There was no happy ending to discover. "It won't, because we're not exhuming anyone."

Dale moved to stand beside his wife. "That's not your decision to make."

"That baby is not Kent," Sophie said. "And I'll prove it. Help me do that, Grant."

Grant didn't make snap decisions. He looked around the room at his married and engaged siblings. He weighed the potential collateral damage and shook his head. He didn't want to chase more ghosts. He wanted to close this chapter of his life and start a new one with Viviana. After everything his family had been through, didn't they all deserve to finally be happy? "No. Every time we dig into this, we find something worse. I won't give Patrice the power to hurt us anymore. I'm done."

Sophie gasped. "How can you say that? Kent is out there."

"He's not, Mom," Grant countered. "It's time to let him go and move on."

"You're wrong," Kenzi interjected angrily. "If you don't care enough to help, Grant, Dax and I will find him."

Dax hugged his wife but said, "I don't think it's that he doesn't care, Kenzi."

She glared up at Dax. "Whose side are you on?"

Lance added, "Everyone understands why you want to believe he's alive, Kenzi. You've always had a fascination with twins. Being one made you feel special. We all want to find him, but—"

Kenzi's face went red. "Oh, my God, you're ready to just give up on him, too? And this isn't about how I feel, this is about Mom. Is it too ugly for you to want to deal with it? You'd rather just sweep it under the rug and pretend we're a perfect family again? When are you going to grow some balls and face that life isn't always pretty?"

Andrew withdrew to the other room with Helene. Ian followed them.

Dax suggested gently, "Kenzi, why don't we step outside for a minute?"

She stepped away from Dax. "You always say you're big on honesty. Well, I'm honestly disappointed that you're not on my side about this."

"Stop," Grant roared in a voice many decibels above anything he'd ever used with his family. "Do you see the destructive potential of going down this road? Look at us, we're already turning on each other. We've come so far. Asher, you have an amazing wife and child. Lance, you and Willa have the twins. Kenzi, I've never seen you happier than you are with Dax. We have too much to lose. Thirty years ago, Patrice nearly destroyed this family. What she did hung over all of us. There is nothing to be gained by learning more. If by some crazy twist it isn't Kent that we buried, what do you think she did with him? I can guarantee you it wasn't good. I want my brother back as much as anyone else, but you know what I don't want? I don't want to trade the chance I have at having a family of my own for what will almost certainly be another disgusting insight into the evil a sociopath is capable of. I love all of you. Don't give one sick woman the power to rip us apart again. Haven't we given her enough?"

A heavy silence hung over the room. Sophie went to Grant and placed a loving hand on his cheek. "I can't move on until I find Kent."

"I understand." Grant placed his hand over his mother's. "But I can't do this for you. I just found out I'm going to be a father with a woman who thinks I don't care, and that's where my time and my energy will be directed. I don't want to live in the past. I choose now. This is where I can make things better. I love you, Mom, but I can't go where you want to take us."

In the background, Kenzi said, "Does it have to be one or the other?"

Grant met her eyes over the head of their mother. "You tell me. If I were you, I wouldn't risk what you have to discover what you probably don't want to know."

Dax took Kenzi's hand. "There is no risk, because I stand with Kenzi no matter where this leads." He arched an eyebrow at Grant. "But it does sound like you need to resolve that other issue before you can do the same."

Sophie lowered her hand to her son's chest above his heart. "You're going to be a father?"

"Yes," he said with a small smile.

"So when is the wedding?" she asked.

Dale interjected, "He might have some convincing to do first."

Sophie searched Grant's face then said, "Thank you for understanding that I'm strong enough that you can be honest with me. You're right. You don't belong here, hunting down what happened a long time ago."

He kissed her cheek softly. "If I thought there was any chance—"

"Go get me my next daughter-in-law and grandchild," his mother said. She looked around, seeming to realize only then that some of her children had left the room. "And thank you for reminding me this has to be done delicately. I will protect my children this time—all of them."

A short time later, Grant was walking down the steps of his parents' house when Kenzi called out to him, "Grant, wait."

He stopped short of his car and turned around. Things had ended on a reasonably good note, and he was happy to leave before the tide turned again. "Yes?"

She rushed toward him with Emily, Willa, and Helene at her heels. "We wanted to talk to you before you left."

We? Oh, God. "Okay."

They made a semi-circle around him, backing him practically up against his car. Willa asked, "Was the woman who rushed out of your office the one who is having your baby?"

"Yes. Her name is Viviana Sutton."

"Why would she think you don't care that she's pregnant?" Helene asked.

"How long have you been seeing her?" Kenzi added.

Emily chimed in. "How far along is she?"

What no chair, ropes, and flashlight? Didn't every interroga-

tion require those? His head was spinning from their questions. "How about if I simply introduce you to her after we work things out?"

Kenzi cocked her head to one side. "She's the reason you've been acting so different lately. It all makes sense now."

"Different?" Grant hedged.

Emily nodded. "Even Asher says he's noticed a change. She's good for you." She smiled. "He said you chewed him out about not telling me where he was going with Andrew. Thank you for that. I love your brother, but he's still rough around the edges."

Feeling more than a little uncomfortable, Grant merely shrugged.

Willa said, "You're always there to take care of everyone else. We wanted you to know you're going to be an incredible father."

"Thank you." *If I shift just a foot over, I can open my car door.*

Helene rubbed her chin. "In nature, animals woo mates in all kinds of ways. Some pound their chests. Some make an attractive nest. Others flaunt bright plumage."

Kenzi's eyebrows came together in concern. "None of them offer to balance each other's checkbooks. Go easy on that."

Grant straightened to his full height, feeling offended. Not one of the women around him seemed the least bit intimidated, though.

Emily added, "She may or may not have health insurance. Don't let that be the first thing you ask her about. You can figure all of that out once you're with her."

"I know how to talk to women," Grant protested.

"Of course you do," Willa said a little too quickly. "We just want this to work out for you."

"So, what's your plan?" Kenzi asked.

A movement in the background caught Grant's attention. His brothers were standing just outside the door with huge smiles on their faces. Even Dax. When they realized he saw them there, they waved and retreated back into the house. *Cowards.*

"I thought I would drive down to see her," Grant said.

"And?" Kenzi prodded.

"Tell her that hearing she's pregnant moved up my timetable of seeing her again."

All four women shook their heads in an eerily synchronized manner.

"Don't say that," Emily said.

Helene added, "Yeah, that's bad."

"But it did. I knew that hearing about Kent would shake the family up. I wanted to wait until that had passed before calling her."

"How did you leave things with her?" Kenzi asked. "What was the last conversation you had?"

He cringed. "It wasn't good. She came to my office, but all the shit was hitting the fan then, and I may have offended her by being too honest about how we met."

"How did you meet?" Emily asked.

Leaving out the storage room details, Grant briefly outlined what had sent him out that night in search of regular people. "Marc said it was vital I learn how the average person speaks."

Willa gasped and asked, "And that's what you told her?"

"I was attempting to explain—"

Kenzi turned to the other women. "He didn't mean it in a bad way. Grant is the most grounded of my brothers. He just doesn't sound it sometimes."

"I'm perfectly capable of speaking for myself," Grant protested.

Emily folded her arms across her chest. "What do you like about this woman, Grant?"

There was so much, he wasn't sure where to start. "She's smart. Funny. Spirited. When I'm with her I like who I am and how she makes me feel."

Willa continued to look him over with a critical eye. "That's better, but if she went to see him to tell him about the baby and he dismissed her as average . . ."

"I didn't dismiss her. She ran off. I was simply explaining—" He reviewed the conversation they'd had and stopped. *Shit.* "Oh, my God. She must think I'm an asshole."

"Probably," Helene agreed. "But on the good side, you're not. So, all we have to do is prove that to her."

"Should we go with him?" Kenzi asked. "Vouch for him?"

Lord save me. "No one is—"

"No, he needs to do this himself for her to respect him," Emily said.

Thank you.

"Do we trust him to not mess this up?" Kenzi asked.

Helene waved a hand in the air. "He was doing something right, or she wouldn't be pregnant."

Enough. Grant opened the door to his car and slid inside. He closed it, but rolled the window down. "I love you all for caring, but I can handle this. I'll call you with an update after we work things out."

Kenzi leaned down next to the window. "Grant, I'm sorry I made it sound like not looking for Kent meant you didn't care. We all know you do."

Grant started his car. "Thank you. I can't straddle both. This is too important to me."

She kissed him on the cheek. "You've got this." She straightened and added, "But call us if things get dicey. And don't talk about money with her. I know you do it because that's how you show you care, but focus on her and the baby. Just keep telling her you care, and it'll work out."

"Tell her you love her," Helene said.

"I'd prefer to wait until I'm certain I feel that way—"

"Don't say that either." Emily waved. "I'll have Asher call you."

"There's no—" *Maybe there is need. After all, he made it to the altar.* "Fine. Now I really do have to go."

He made the mistake of looking into his rearview mirror before he drove off. Although they were all waving goodbye, they each looked concerned enough that he had a moment of doubt.

What if Viviana was too angry to see him?

Male confidence surged forward to save him.

Then I'll just change her mind.

"COME IN," VIVIANA called out while finishing entering an invoice for the rental of a bulldozer in her office trailer. She glanced down at the yellow sundress and sandals she'd purchased on impulse. She'd already found a small apartment of her own and was discovering who she was when she stopped worrying about what she was supposed to be. A year ago sitting at this desk had felt confining, now the familiarity of it brought her comfort. *Being here now is my choice.*

The door opened and Gerald, one of her father's oldest employees, entered. He was past retirement age, but he'd said he had little to go home to and preferred to keep working with a lighter workload. He was presently a glorified delivery man—which sometimes included coffee and lunches—but he never seemed to mind. Retaining Gerald as an employee, even though his most productive years had ended long ago, exemplified what Viviana admired about her father: he was a strong man with a loyal, caring side.

Gerald approached Viviana's desk with a shyness she didn't normally associate with him. "You busy, Viv?"

Viviana turned from her computer and stood. "Never too busy for you, Gerald. What's up?"

He sat in the seat before her desk and smacked his hands on his jean-clad thighs, adding a puff of dust to the office. "Are you looking for a husband?"

Viviana coughed in surprise. "Not right this moment."

Gerald cleared his throat. "Sue Wickers was at the pharmacy when you bought pre-natal vitamins."

With a groan, Viviana sat heavily back onto her seat. *I grew up here. Why did I think for a second I would be as anonymous as I was in Boston?*

Gerald removed his baseball hat, folding and unfolding it in his hands as he continued, "She told Claire at the donut shop. Claire's son, James, is graduating from college this year with a master's degree in education. She asked me if there was a father in the picture because her son has always had a sweet spot for you. I said I didn't know. I hadn't heard that you were expecting. I said you might have been buying the vitamins for a friend. No one is looking to upset you, but a couple of the crew might also toss their hat into the ring if you've found yourself in a difficult situation and it's something you're not wanting to go through alone."

Viviana didn't say anything at first as she rode out a wave of sheer embarrassment. If Gerald knew, then everyone in town knew. And, apparently, there was a mortifying number who felt sorry enough for her to make this even more awkward. "That's so generous of everyone, but I'm fine."

Gerald made a pained face. "I've made you feel bad. I didn't mean to. I'd offer to marry you myself if I were forty years younger."

Oh. Now I'm going to cry. Viviana went over to sit in the chair beside him. Gerald didn't have a mean bone in his body, and he wasn't one to talk about this kind of thing. He was there because he cared. She gave him what she hoped was her sweetest smile. "And I would have scared the shit out of you by accepting."

He cackled at that then became serious again. "Are you really pregnant, Viv?"

"Yes. It wasn't something I was going to announce yet, though."

"And the baby's daddy?"

Someone else might have found his questions impolite, but Viviana had grown up with him. Half the swears she knew she'd learned from following him around the site. "He won't be in the picture."

"Then he's a fucking idiot," Gerald announced.

"Yes," Viviana agreed, even though that wasn't the way she wanted to remember him. She was still trying not to think of him at all. "Tell everyone they don't have to worry about me, though. I'm doing okay. Hard as it may be to believe, I missed your sorry asses, and I'm happy to be back."

Gerald cackled again. "Not surprising at all, some of us have mighty fine asses regardless of our ages."

Viviana laughed at that. There was a fun swagger to the men she'd grown up around. It was harmless and something she hadn't realized was so funny until it hadn't been part of her life anymore. She sat back with a smile and reflected on what he'd come to tell her. "Could you also please spread the message that, although the idea of sympathy proposals is sweet, they're not necessary?"

Looking her straight in the eye, Gerald asked seriously, "What sympathy are you talking about? Half the men in town have been mooning over you since you kicked their butts in high school. They've been panting for you to have a reason you might need one of them. Strength in a woman is good, but you've been so damned independent for so long, none of them thought they had anything to offer you."

"Independent? I was living with my dad until I moved away."

"Because you give all your money to the Cairo Mercy Foundation. You're softhearted. There's a lot of people in this town who are grateful to you for what you've done for them through those grants."

"Their gratitude belongs with my mother. She founded it."

"But you've funded it."

Viviana shrugged. "Sometimes. Mostly it is self-sufficient since people pay back into it when they can."

"James used a grant from the foundation to finish college. Now he's coming home single and grateful. Rumor is he's handsome, too."

Oh, boy. "I'm not looking for a husband, Gerry."

"But would you be offended by some flowers? A few date requests? I'm only asking you because people keep asking me."

Her first reaction was to say no, but she didn't voice it. *Why not? I'm single.* She couldn't imagine feeling anything for anyone, but she'd told herself her return home wasn't a defeat. *So, why hang my head and hide?* "I've never gotten flowers," she said honestly. "That might actually be nice."

Gerald nodded, stood, and replaced his hat. "I'll pass the word."

Viviana almost told him not to. She wavered on whether or not she wanted to open that door, but she reminded herself of something Audrey had once said, "The best way to get over a man is to find a new one."

Memories of how it had been to be with Grant tumbled through her thoughts. Even as she said goodbye to Gerald, she fought to push back a yearning she told herself was a waste of time. *Don't think about him. When it was good it wasn't real, and when it was real it definitely wasn't good.*

Let him go.

Chapter Twelve

Dressed in jeans and a T-shirt, Grant stopped at a florist shop on his drive from a small private airfield to Cairo, New York where Viviana lived. He'd had a rental car delivered and told his helicopter pilot to not expect to hear from him until the next day. He was feeling confident when he walked up to the cashier and asked, "What kind of bouquet do you give a woman to subtly announce that your intentions are serious?"

The short, middle-aged, redhead with a thousand freckles and a huge smile, called to the backroom, "Looks like we've got another one."

"Another one?" Grant asked. Although he'd given flowers to women in the past, he'd always had his secretary order them. Walking into a florist shop himself was part of what made the trip more exciting. *I'm out here with regular people doing regular things.*

And I like it.

"Sorry," the redhead said with a laugh. "You look like a rose man. Big white roses. Maybe two dozen."

Grant nodded.

Her smile widened. "Or four. Four dozen definitely makes a statement."

He pictured the size of that bouquet. "You don't think that's too big?"

"Not when you're telling a woman how you feel. We have packages that include custom delivery options."

"I'll be delivering them myself."

"Okay," the woman said while writing up the order. "It'll take a few minutes."

As Grant waited he looked around the shop. It was surprisingly sparse on flowers. Normally, he would have taken the time to advise the owner on the benefit to keeping the shelves properly stocked and walk him or her through tax write-off procedures. Many people were unaware of how all the small deductions could add up and help them raise revenue they could then reinvest into their business. *Not today. Today, I'm just a man driving into town to see a woman.*

A woman who is having my baby.

I can't mess this up.

For just a second he found it hard to breathe as he remembered how hurt she'd looked when she ran from him. *She could hate me, and she wouldn't be wrong to.*

He paid for the flowers and exceeded the speed limit as he drove the rest of the way to her office. It was his best guess on where she would be. In the past he wouldn't have gone in blind, but he didn't want to use a private investigator or his security team for this. *When something is this important, you do it yourself.*

He drove up to a trailer that had a sign "Sutton Con-

171

struction and Rental Main Office" on it. He grabbed the huge bouquet of flowers and made his way up the steps of the trailer. Part of him wanted to throw the door open and enter with bravado. Another part of him thought it would be a good idea to wait until he knew if she was even in there. He knocked because a sign beside the door instructed him to.

"Come in," Viviana said from inside.

Before opening the door he held the flowers behind his back, changed his mind and held them in front of him, then switched them to behind him again. With a shake of his head and a deep indrawn breath, he opened the door.

The first thing he noticed was how shocked Viviana looked to see him. He searched her face for joy. If it was there, it was hidden well. He let the door close behind him.

The second thing he noticed was that the office was full of all kinds of flowers. There were three vases of them on her desk, several on the floor around her desk, and even more on a nearby conference table. He forced a smile and held out his bouquet toward her. "Hi."

She stood. "What are you doing here?"

Rather than answering, he picked up a card that was beside one of the vases of flowers. HAVE DINNER WITH ME, KEVIN. "Who is Kevin?"

She strode over and took the card away from him. "None of your business."

What he hadn't expected was the rush of possessiveness that filled him. He was known for being rational and calm. Imagining her with another man made him want to stomp his feet and pound his chest like some caveman before hauling her off somewhere so he could remind her why she belonged with him. He was wise enough, though, not to share those thoughts with her. He picked up another card and read it. CALL ME, JAMES. It included his number. "They're not all from the same man?"

Viviana ripped that card away from him as well. "Do you mind?"

I do, actually. I mind all of this. He walked over and picked up another card. Viviana took it away from him before he had a chance to read it, but he'd held it long enough to see it was from still another man. "What's going on here?"

She walked around the room, collected all the cards, then stuffed them in her desk drawer. "Nothing that has anything to do with you. We've already said everything we have to say to each other."

No, my little Viv, we have not. Grant laid his bouquet of flowers on the front of her desk and took a moment to assess the situation. None of the cards had been a thank you for a great night with her. They had sounded like invitations. "Come here," he said.

She shook her head and stayed behind her desk. "No. Listen we had fun together. That's it. I'm not even upset anymore about what you said in your office. I just want to put it all behind me."

"Liar." He stepped closer to her, leaning over the desk and bracing himself on both hands. He ignored the flowers that flanked him on the left side. They were no more of a threat than the men who had sent them. Now that he was with her again there was no denying the sexual attraction that pulsed between them. She felt it, too. It was there in her eyes. He'd seen that look several times since he'd met her, and it usually led somewhere decadent. "We did have fun, but something that intense shouldn't end over a misunderstanding."

Her chest rose and fell, and he wondered if she, too, was imagining him taking her on the desk. The vases would hit the floor just before he slid that sundress strap over her shoulder. His name would be the name she cried out as he pushed her dress up and plunged inside her.

"I understood you perfectly, and that's why I think you should leave now."

Okay, so, she needs to hear me say it. "When I called you average and ordinary—"

"Get out," she said harshly.

"I wasn't slumming. Not by your definition of the word. Yes, I was out that night looking for someone from a lower socio-economic circle."

She picked up her phone. "If you don't leave now, I will call the police. Or my family. Honestly, the police would treat you better."

He straightened. She looked serious. "If you hear me out, I believe you'll see—"

She raised a finger above the phone pad as if she were about to make one of those calls. "I didn't ask you to come here. Go back to Boston. We have nothing left to say to each other."

"I—" She tapped a number into the phone.

He raised both hands in the air. His goal wasn't to end up on the evening news. "Okay. Okay. I'm going."

She was glaring at him when he turned to leave. She was still glaring at him when he looked over his shoulder before he opened the door. *That's not good. Maybe I should call Asher.*

Grant was still standing outside the trailer when an older man approached him. "What are you doing here, son?" the man asked.

"I'm here to see Viviana." Because there was no better way to describe their relationship, he added, "I'm a friend from Boston."

The man stepped closer. "A friend from Boston?"

"Yes."

"Grant Barrington?"

"Yes," Grant said in relief. If this man knew him by name, then he knew how ridiculous it would be to involve the police. "That's me."

"I've heard about you." That's all the man said before he struck Grant in the nose.

Grant stumbled backward against the steps beneath the surprisingly powerful punch. "What the hell?" Grant roared.

The door of the trailer crashed open. "Oh, no. Gerald, don't hurt him. He's from the *city*."

She said the last part like it equated to him having never taken a punch in his life. He had, of course. Normally, though, it was from someone he was paying to hone his skills and not a sneak attack from another person he couldn't in good conscience strike back. "I'm fine," he said grumpily.

"You're bleeding," Viviana exclaimed. She rushed to his side. "He broke your nose."

"Nah, I barely touched him. His face will still be just as pretty once the swelling goes down," Gerald said smugly.

"Gerald," Viviana admonished, "he was leaving. I had it under control."

"Ow," Grant said simply to test a theory.

Viviana's attention swung back to him, and she had the most adorable worried expression on her face. It was almost worth the throbbing headache he was now sporting. She slid under one of his arms, prepared to take the weight of him if he couldn't walk. "Are you dizzy? Can you walk? Come back inside."

At least she's not calling the police anymore. "I'm fine, but I wouldn't mind stepping out of the heat for a minute with a paper towel," he said, but hugged her close to his side simply because she felt so good against him. This time it was the old man who was glaring at him while he walked away, and Grant took that as a sign that things were turning around.

Once inside the office trailer, Viviana guided him to a chair then quickly returned with several paper towels, some wet, some dry. Grant cleaned off his face. Thankfully his nose had almost instantly stopped bleeding. Gerald was accurate in his guess that it was sore and likely swollen, but not broken.

Viviana paced beside his chair. "You shouldn't have come here."

"I had to," he said.

She stopped and put a hand on one of her hips. "Why?"

He stood and tossed the paper towels in a trash bin before answering. He considered being completely upfront with her, but remembered what Kenzi and the others had thought of that idea. He didn't normally dance around a subject as big as the fact that she was carrying his baby and he had a right to know.

Maybe some arguments, though, were like chess competitions—winning didn't matter as much as everyone leaving it with what they needed. *What does she need from me? Kenzie said to just keep telling her I care.*

Could it be that simple? "I care about you, and I knew you'd been hurt by what I said." He could have tried to explain again that his comment, if heard in the context of what was going on in his life, actually wasn't an insult—but he didn't choose to defend himself. One day soon, when he woke to find her cuddled to his side, he would tell her everything. For now, it was better to keep things simple. "I'm sorry I hurt you. I didn't mean to."

She expelled a heartfelt sigh. "It didn't have to end that way."

"It doesn't have to end at all. Not if we don't want it to."

She turned away and covered her face with both hands. He went to stand behind her. "Sometimes what we think we want isn't what's best for us."

Gently he encircled her waist with his arms and pulled her back against him. "How will we know unless we try?"

She leaned her head back against his shoulder. "Oh, no. I'm not falling for that logic twice. That's what got me into this mess."

His hand naturally sought her still flat stomach. "What mess?"

She tensed and he waited.

THERE WAS SOMETHING so wrong and so right about being in Grant's arms again. It was difficult to convince her body he was the source of her nervousness rather than her comfort.

I shouldn't have gone after him. I should have let him take a punch and leave. The longer he stays the harder it is to remember why I can't tell him about the baby.

Without the baby, would I already be kissing him, giving myself over to how he makes me feel? Am I so weak that I might slip up and go that route regardless?

How would he react to the news?

Would he run back to Boston, hoping I don't have the nerve to follow?

Would he want joint custody?

How would that work with a man I hardly know?

She turned in his arms and tilted her face back so she could see his expression. *Are you a good man, Grant Barrington? If I tell you, will you treasure this baby?*

Just then the door of her office flew open and her brother, Dylan, said, "Now can we kill him?"

Viviana stepped out of Grant's arms and moved in front of him. "No one is killing anyone." Although she tried to sound confident, she shivered with apprehension when Connor came in, followed by her father. "Dad, don't do anything rash."

Her father nodded, but walked up to Grant. "Is this him?"

"Yes. He came by to apologize." She had no idea how her father would react to meeting him since they were entering into uncharted territory. What she did know, though, was if she did tell him about the baby, she didn't want to do it like this.

"Well, that's a start," her father said as he held out his hand to Grant. "I'm Sean Sutton. Viviana's father. You must be Grant Barrington."

Grant winced then shook his hand. "Yes, that's me."

The two men took a moment to size each other up. Her father had the strength of a man who worked hard, but Grant matched him in height and breadth of shoulders. Dylan and Connor flanked their father and Viviana was pleasantly surprised when Grant didn't seem intimidated by them, either. They were a formidable wall of muscle most men backed down from.

"Long drive from Boston?" her father asked when he released Grant's hand.

"I flew in," Grant answered. When her father seemed to be waiting for more information, Grant added, "By helicopter to Marsh Airfield."

"Helicopter? Really? What kind?" Connor asked.

Dylan punched him in the arm. "It doesn't matter."

Viviana closed her eyes briefly. She usually found her brothers' antics amusing, but not at that moment.

Her father asked, "So, you're leaving tonight?"

Grant shrugged. "My plan was to stay . . . in a local hotel

if I could find one."

"No longer necessary," her father answered without hesitation. "Any friend of Viviana's should stay at the main house. There's plenty of empty rooms. Especially now that Viviana lives on her own."

Why, why didn't I tell my father that Grant doesn't know?

Oh, yeah, because he wouldn't have agreed with that decision.

"Dad, he was only joking. He's not staying."

Dylan chimed in as well. "Bad idea, Dad. We don't know him."

"You a thief?" Her father pinned down Grant with one of his most intimidating looks.

"No, sir," Grant answered with just enough respect that her father relaxed somewhat.

"Then unless you give me a reason to change my mind, my home is open to you. Why don't we all have dinner together tonight and get to know each other? We have a lot to talk about."

No, Dad. No. Viviana said, "I'm sure Grant—"

"Thank you," Grant said. "And dinner sounds lovely. I always enjoy sampling someone else's chef's dishes."

An awkward silence followed. Viviana's eyes flew to Grant's. Was he making fun of her family? She said, "The chef's name changes nightly at our house. I believe tonight is Connor's turn so we're probably having pizza again."

"Oh, of course." Grant's expression looked like a man who'd just realized he sounded pretentious. "I like pizza."

"I'm sure," Dylan countered with narrowed eyes. "Rats

love cheese."

Rats? What was Dylan talking about?

Grant shook his head as if denying an accusation that Viviana had somehow missed. Had they been alone, she would have asked Grant about it, but right then she was more concerned with finding a way to stop Grant from getting so cozy with her father. *If I can get a moment alone with him, I'm sure I can make him see how insane of an idea that is.*

"Don't you have somewhere to be, Dad? You're scheduled for a roof appraisal in Greenville. It's a half hour out and then back. If you're shooting to be home for dinner you'd better get going."

Her father kissed her cheek then gave Grant one last, measured look. "I'll be back in a couple hours."

One down. Viviana turned to her brothers. "The highway department is done with the dump truck. It needs to be picked up, cleaned, and checked if it's going out again tomorrow."

Dylan looked at Connor. "I dropped it off."

Connor shook his head. "I'm not picking it up and doing maintenance on it."

Their father added, "Go together. Someone needs to drive the car back. Clean it while you look it over, and you'll be back at the house by seven."

They grumbled but agreed.

A few minutes later, Viviana found herself alone with Grant again. "I'll explain to my family that you had some kind of emergency and had to return to Boston."

He turned and stepped closer to her, close enough that she found it difficult to concentrate on anything beyond how her body began to hum for him. "I'm staying."

I knew you'd say that.

Oh, God.

"I'm pregnant," she blurted.

"I know," he answered without blinking.

She couldn't remember ever getting as angry as fast as she did just then. "*How* do you know?" *Audrey?*

"How doesn't matter. What does matter is I'm here, and I want to give us a chance, Viviana." He ran his hands up and down her arms in a comforting fashion that only fanned her temper.

"There isn't an us." Her head was spinning. If he already knew, that meant he was there *because* he'd found out.

"There is if you want there to be."

Because of the baby.

His face blurred as tears filled Viviana's eyes. She picked up a vase of flowers. "I'm sorry, but I've reached my max on men who are interested in me only since they've heard I'm pregnant." She smashed the vase on the floor. "I don't need anyone who didn't want me before." She picked up another vase and smashed that one on the floor as well. "I don't want to date them." She sent another vase to the ground. "I don't want to marry them." And another. "This was supposed to make me feel better, but all it's done is make me feel worse. I don't want pity, and I don't need a man to take care of me." She sent one final vase crashing to the floor then stood there, breathing heavily, not caring what Grant thought of her.

She was so angry she was shaking.

He wrapped his arms around her and simply held her. She wanted to hate his touch. Her brain told her to pull away and ask him what part of what she'd said hadn't been in English. Instead, she laid her head on his, even while her fisted hands struck at his back.

Finally, when she quieted, he kissed the top of her head and said, "The last thing I want to do is hurt you more. Hear me out just once, then if you want me to leave, I will. I will want to stay in touch because I cannot imagine not being part of my child's life, but we'll do it in a way you're comfortable with."

Adrenaline spent, Viviana nodded and let herself savor what might be the last time in his arms. "I'm listening." *Kind of. God, he feels so good.*

His heart beat loudly in his chest while he took a moment to choose his words. "You once told me you went to Boston because you needed to discover who you really were. I had been asked to do something for my family that required I leave my office and talk to people. Regular people. I don't know if you've realized this about me, but that's not an area I excel at."

Despite how she tried to keep the walls around her heart, they started to crumble as he opened up to her. This was the man she'd laughed with, trusted, started to fall for. "You could start by not calling them regular."

He tucked her head under his chin and hugged her closer. "Noted. But when I call you regular, I mean real, grounded, honest. It's not an insult. So many people in my circle pretend to be something they aren't. You're you, and that's pretty incredible. This life you have here is what I've always imagined average Americans liv—"

"Average is actually more offensive than regular."

"I see," he stopped, then sighed. "I didn't realize how isolated my life had become before I met you. I went to work. I went home. Yes, I saw my family and met my social commitments, but there were no surprises—at least, not good ones anyway."

She eased back and placed a hand over her stomach. "You consider this a good surprise?"

He laid his hand over hers. "Don't you?"

She started to shake again as emotions rushed through her. "I do, but I'm realistic. Neither of us planned this. That's why I didn't tell you."

He raised her chin so her eyes met his. "No, you didn't tell me because you thought I was an asshole."

"I don't know you well enough to know what I think of you."

He kissed her briefly, gently on the lips. "Then let's change that."

She wasn't ready to throw caution to the wind and believe in what he was offering. "For the baby's sake."

A smile tugged at one side of his mouth. "And for mine. My life was boring before you. Don't send me back to it." He kissed her gently again. "That would be cruel."

She studied his face, looking for any hint of insincerity but found none. "Although it's flattering to imagine I'm interesting enough to keep around—I don't know what that would look like or if I could agree to something like that right now."

"Not interesting—captivating." He ran a hand through her hair. "As far as what it would look like, I've heard of this thing people do when they want to get to know each other better—I believe they call it dating."

He said it with such a straight face that for a second she thought he was serious, then she saw the laughter in his eyes. She smiled and swatted his arm. "Jerk."

"Say yes, Viv."

"To start dating now, after we've already made a baby? I don't know." It seemed like too big of a decision to make hastily. This wasn't saying yes to a drink with a stranger at a bar. It wasn't agreeing to go to the movies with someone she'd just met. This was the father of the child she was carrying. If he wanted to be an important part of their child's life, that meant he would be part of her life—always. Was it better to try to move forward as friends or give this another try?

What if round two ended worse than round one had? Where would that leave them? What would it mean for their child? She asked, "Why did you say yes to staying at my father's place?"

His eyes darkened. "Because if we marry they'll be my family."

Marry? Holy shit, that's where he sees this going? No. He didn't say when, he said if. He doesn't know either. "They don't like you."

"Yet," he said with a confidence she envied.

There was a knock on the door. Gerald popped his head in. His eyes widened when he saw broken glass and flowers everywhere. "Everything okay in here?"

She blushed. "I was wrong, Gerry. I guess I didn't want the flowers."

"Guess not," he said. "And him?"

"We're still figuring that out," she said as much to Grant as to Gerald.

Grant put his arm around her waist.

Gerald's eyes narrowed. He looked around the trashed room again. Viviana saw the room through his eyes and rushed to say, "I did that. Not him."

Gerald nodded. "I hope so. Funny thing about small towns, Grant Barrington: we protect our own. You remember that."

After Gerald left, Grant joked, "I was sure he was going to threaten to use some large machinery to bury me in the back like your brothers did."

Viviana's head snapped back. "When did my brothers say that?" He didn't need to say anything to guess what had happened. "I'm going to kill them."

"No," Grant said. "If you want there to be any chance of them accepting me, let it go."

I don't know if I can. "Rats like cheese. Dylan thought you'd already ratted him out for telling you I was pregnant."

"I'm taking the fifth on all of this, so it's not a lie when you say you didn't hear it from me. Especially if they'll be sleeping down the hall from me. They do both still live with your father, don't they?"

"Yes, they do."

Grant rubbed his jaw as if it were tender.

Anger surged in Viviana again. "Did one of them hit you?" Grant said nothing but he didn't have to. Her brothers were hotheads, which was why she hadn't told them when, Sidney, her ex-boyfriend had stolen from her. "I almost called the police on you, but so far you're the one with reason to."

He shook his head. "Who knows, given similar circumstances I might have done the same."

"You don't have to say that. I know they're meatheads. I love them, but that doesn't mean I'm not aware of their . . . more impulsive side."

"I have brothers I feel the same way about. That's something else we have in common."

He meant it. She could see it in his eyes. "In Boston, I did think you were an asshole."

He smiled. "I know."

It was scary to lower her guard once she'd raised it. "I didn't in the beginning. When we first met I saw you more like this."

He pressed his lips together briefly before answering. "They're both me. I'm not perfect, Viviana. I work too much. I don't have friends because I never made time for them. According to the women in my family there is an inevitability to me offending you, despite their guidance. That's me."

"Your family knows about me?" she asked, swallowing hard.

"Just the basics," he said, looking briefly down at her stomach then up again.

"I bet I know what they think of me."

He ran his hand through her hair again. "I bet you don't. If I survive your family, I'll introduce you to mine. Then we'll call it even."

She chuckled. "That bad?"

He shrugged. "They can be, but things have been better lately. You'll understand once you meet them." After a pause, he looked around at the mess. "So, should we warn the cleaning crew about the glass?"

Viviana blinked a few times, half expecting him to start laughing. When he didn't she went over to the closet, retrieved a dustpan and broom, then handed him the broom and said, "Watch out for the glass *we* need to pick up."

"Of course." He looked at the broom as if it were a complicated gadget, and he needed a moment to figure it out. Then he smiled and started sweeping up larger pieces. "This isn't so bad."

He looked so adorably proud of himself, Viviana burst out laughing. He started laughing along with her. For a moment, they were back to who they had been when they'd first met, two people simply enjoying each other, before everything got complicated.

Viviana went up on her toes and kissed his smiling lips. They both froze. She stepped back. "Let's do it. Let's date."

"Sounds good," he said in a strangled voice before returning to the task of sweeping the glass into a pile.

Desire licked through her, held in check only by their

location. A heated look from him said he was waging the same inner battle.

Viviana instinctively placed her hand over her stomach. *Please. Please let this be the right choice for all of us.* "Want to see what we do here?" she asked in place of the other questions racing through her head.

"Sure."

She led the way out of the trailer. The two of them stood for a moment at the bottom of the steps. Some of the crew were returning equipment and paused to watch. One had sent her flowers that day. Would they accept Grant?

Viviana glanced at him then back at the crew. *They'll have to because this is not their choice to make, it's mine.* Working in construction had taught her the greatest risk of getting hurt came from half-assing something. She squared her shoulders and took Grant's hand in hers.

Okay. Here we go.

Chapter Thirteen

GRANT FINISHED ANOTHER beer then reached for more pizza, but he doubted he could eat it. His sides hurt from laughing so hard. Viviana's family was fucking hilarious, even when they didn't mean to be.

Or I've had too much alcohol.

No, they're funny.

The initially tense meal had started with Viviana explaining to her family that they'd decided to try to work things out. A brief interrogation followed that he thought he'd handled well.

What did Grant do for a living? The pointed questions her father followed up with revealed two things: Sean Sutton was an intelligent man who understood more than he let on.

How would he navigate working in Boston and dating someone three hours away? Easy. Helicopter. Saves time.

Things got a little dicey when Dylan asked him what his favorite beer was, and he explained he wasn't a big drinker.

"That's because you've never tasted our homemade brew," Connor had said gleefully, which perhaps should have made Grant question his motives.

Instead Grant had said, "I'd love to try it."

One beer had led to two then three. Viviana, water in hand, had warned him to slow down, but Grant had felt like he'd stepped into an improv skit where the instructions had been to one up each other with embarrassing stories. Connor did an impression of Dylan that was so spot on Grant almost spit out a mouthful of beer when he heard it. Dylan told a story about how Viviana had been tougher than Connor when they were little. When a bully had started harassing Connor in middle school, ten-year-old Viviana had confronted the boy and kicked his butt.

Which, according to Dylan, begged two questions: How tough could that bully have been if he got his ass handed to him by a ten-year-old girl, and if Connor was once that much of a pussy was he destined to always be one?

Viviana had rolled her eyes at his comment, but she didn't seem offended by the comment. Grant had looked at Sean to see his reaction, but rather than looking disappointed as his father would have, Viviana's father laughed as he told his son to watch his language.

Viviana had chimed in then with a retelling of the time Dylan had pretended to be too sick to go to school because a girl in his class had said she wanted to kiss him. She and Connor had high fived over the table, and Dylan glared at them for a second before laughing along.

Grant had laughed too and had another beer.

The room spun a little, but Grant was enjoying himself too much to mind. He slapped his hand down on the table and declared, "I love this family."

Dylan laughed. "Oh, man, he really is a lightweight."

Viviana slapped her brother's arm. "He told you he doesn't drink."

"If he hugs me can I punch him?" Connor asked.

Grant chuckled at that. Yes, he knew they were talking about him like he wasn't there, but they were just too funny.

"Touch him and you die," Viviana threatened. "Dad, tell them to stop. He's important to me."

I'm important to her. Grant swayed a little in his chair and gave her a goofy smile.

Suddenly Viviana looked concerned. "Did you spike his beer with your home-brewed grain alcohol as well?" She slammed the pizza box closed. "That's it. Party's over. I'm leaving, and I'm taking him with me."

Her father said, "He stays here."

A blurry Viviana went toe to toe with her equally blurry father. "No. You've just proven I can't trust you with him."

Grant tried to tell her it was no big deal, but his words came out slurred. *So this is how drunk feels.* Like a child who had imbibed in too many sweets and made himself sick, Grant shared a guilty look with her brothers. "Are we in trouble? She looks pissed," he whispered.

Dylan said, "We are, and she is." Her brothers roared with laughter. Grant tried not to, but he joined in.

Viviana's voice rose. "Dad, I'm serious. This isn't a joke to me. I came home because I missed all of you, but this will never happen again." With hands on her hips, she waved a finger at her brothers. "Never, do you hear me? No matter how things work out between us, Grant will always be the father of my child, and you will either treat him with respect or you won't be part of our lives."

She is so fucking beautiful when she's angry.

And, man, is she angry.

"Now, Dad, help me get him into my car. We'll drive him to my place and put him on the couch. And then, tomorrow morning, I want Connor and Dylan at my house apologizing." She sniffed and suddenly looked like she might cry. "Tonight was important to me. I'm disappointed in all of you."

Never had Grant ever felt more like an ass.

From the way her brothers hung their heads they felt the same.

"I'm sorry," Grant mumbled. He tried to stand, but his legs wobbled beneath him. Normally he would have been upset at the idea of someone making him look foolish, but when he met her brothers' eyes they all burst out laughing again.

One day, this might be a story they shared about him. The idea was strangely pleasing. He tried to explain that to both Viviana and her father as they drove him to her place, but neither paid much attention to what he was saying.

They sent him into the bathroom, gave him water and Tylenol, then tucked him into the couch with a blanket and pillow. Viviana took a seat in the chair across from him.

"I'm sure he's fine, but I'll stay up to make sure he's okay," she said to her father.

Grant smiled at her.

She didn't smile back.

Her father took a seat in the chair beside her. "I'll stay as well."

Grant's eyes began to flutter and close. The last thing he said before he gave in to sleep was, "Your family is awesome, and I think I might love you."

DINNER WITH HER family hadn't gone at all the way Viviana had hoped it would. *Disaster* was an understatement.

If I were a person who believed in signs, I would say this relationship has not received the approval from above. So far my family has threatened Grant, assaulted him, and now potentially given him alcohol poisoning. He might think he loves me now, but when he wakes with a killer hangover and the clarity of a sober mind, he'll see he doesn't and run back to Boston. And I won't even blame him. She sighed.

"It's all going to be okay, baby," her father said from the chair beside her.

Viviana crossed her arms in front of her. "No, Dad, I don't think so. Not this time." *I might as well tell him the truth.* "I hadn't told Grant I was pregnant. I thought he wasn't a good enough person to be part of this baby's life. I had it all wrong. Look at *us*. We'll be lucky if he doesn't fight me for custody, and he'd have a good case for it. Why did I think I could do this? What do I know about being a mother?"

"Stop. We're good people. Nothing that happened tonight has anything to do with your ability to be a good mother. Your brothers had a little fun hazing your new boyfriend; any man you end up with needs to be able to handle them."

"Gerald almost broke Grant's nose."

Her father coughed back a laugh.

Viviana's temper flared again. "I wish I could laugh with you. This is not Scott Mead backing out of taking me to prom because Dylan and Connor threatened to break his legs if he even held my hand. I don't know if Grant is the man for me, but I want the chance to find out. I don't want to have to choose between here and happiness."

"Is that the choice you feel you're being given?"

"Tonight, yes. I love it here, Dad, but I'm not sixteen anymore. If you're here tonight to make sure I don't sleep with him again, I need to tell you that's the least of what you should be worried about." Tears filled her eyes. "I'm ready to cry again, and you know I'm not a crier. I don't know what I'm supposed to do. I've never felt so happy and sad at the same time. I go back and forth between hopeful and scared out of my mind. All I'm asking is for you to respect the decisions I make. I may make all the wrong ones, but even the right ones won't work out if you all sabotage them."

Her father said nothing for a few minutes. When he spoke his tone was deep with emotion. "I wish you could remember your mother when she was healthy. She had a way of cutting through crap and refocusing me on what's important. I see her in you so often. Your brothers didn't mean any harm, but I'll talk to them. We'd all like to see you with a husband and family. Or single if that's what you decide."

"Thank you."

"Just to clear the air, Connor confessed to me they went

to Boston to threaten Grant. Dylan admitted he clocked him as well."

Viviana covered her face with her hands. "Oh, my God. Grant needs to take a self-defense course just to visit me."

"I've been looking into your boyfriend. I don't think he's not retaliating because he doesn't know how."

It was an odd enough comment that Viviana lowered her hands and looked over at her father. "What are you saying?"

"Not sure if it's a good or bad thing that you don't know."

"I don't understand."

"He's an extremely wealthy man, Viv. Money like that can be a dangerous thing. There is more to him than he's showing us. How did the two of you meet?"

"We were both running by the Charles." The truth, just the tamest part of it.

"Have you known him long?"

She looked away, made a face, then met her father's gaze. "Not really."

Her father didn't say anything, but he didn't have to. She'd thought the same thing about a hundred times since she'd discovered she was pregnant. She looked across at the slumbering, snoring man sprawled out on her couch. "We're giving us a chance, although I don't know why he's trying as hard as he is."

"You're not giving yourself or us much credit. If he wins your heart there are plenty in this town who will think he's one lucky bastard."

Viviana smiled at that. "I did get a good share of flowers

today."

Her father nodded. "Of course you did, baby. Grant is no fool. He sees the same wonderful woman the rest of the town sees. If he forgets that when he wakes up, I'll remind him. I don't want to be the only Sutton who hasn't hit him."

"Dad," Viviana exclaimed.

Her father chuckled. "I'm kidding. Connor hasn't yet, either."

Viviana rolled her eyes skyward. "Not funny."

Her father pinched the air. "Not even a little?"

"Too soon."

"I don't think you have to worry about Grant." Her father relaxed deeper in his chair. "What you've got there is a strong man who wants to be part of this family rather than steal you away from us."

"So strong a seventy-year-old man can almost knock him over?"

"No, so strong he let him."

Viviana took a moment to digest that. "You like him."

"I'm reserving my opinion for after I know him better. Your brothers are, too, but he improved the chances of us approving of him by acting the way he did tonight. I know you imagined tonight differently, but men have their own way of figuring each other out. You'll see. Tomorrow they'll all be friendly."

Moments from the evening flashed in Viviana's mind. Grant laughing along with her brothers. Him whispering to them. Them whispering back. "I hope you're right."

In the quiet that followed, Viviana's eyes began to flutter

and close.

"Viv?" her father prompted.

"Yeah, Dad?"

"I'm not here as a chaperone."

"No?"

"I'm here because you said he's important to you—that makes him important to me, too. You were right—no matter what happens between the two of you, that man will be the father of my grandbaby. He's family now."

Viviana let her eyes close and nodded. *Family.*

Her mind drifted off to a place where she and Grant were married and chasing children out the door to go to school. It was such a good dream she didn't want to wake from it even when the sound of her apartment door opening and closing almost woke her.

Chapter Fourteen

GRANT WOKE TO a thudding headache and a carpeted tongue. Although he'd heard people moan about hangovers, he'd never actually experienced one. Why would anyone voluntarily put themselves through this?

And who knew beer had that kind of kick?

He opened one eye, peered at the ceiling, and groaned as his stomach dangerously churned. *I hope this bedroom has a bathroom attached.* Turning his head, he forgot about how he felt when he saw Viviana asleep in a chair a few feet away. *I'm not in a bed, am I? I'm on a couch.*

With Viviana?

Her eyes opened. "Hey."

"Hey," he croaked. "Are we still at your dad's?"

"No, we're at my place. You got wrecked last night so I brought you here."

He looked down and saw that outside of his shoes, he was still fully dressed. "Sorry. I don't usually drink and when I do it's one or two. I guess I had five too many. I don't remember a lot of last night. That's never happened to me before."

"I'm the one who's sorry." She pushed a stray curl out of her face and grimaced. "My brothers thought it would be funny to introduce you to homemade grain alcohol."

"The beer was spiked?" He remembered thinking the beer had more of a punch to it than he'd expected. Now the experience made sense. He was accustomed to being able to anticipate the actions of most people, but the Suttons were like dealing with feral cats. He only knew about cats because he'd once dated a woman who rescued them. Domesticated cats preened and purred. Feral cats were unpredictable and made walking by something as innocent looking as a couch potentially dangerous for the ankles.

I always kind of preferred the latter. It kept things interesting.

Grant pushed himself up to a seated position. Only then did he realize how closely Viviana was watching him. He might have been able to guess what she wanted from him if he wasn't concentrating so hard on not throwing up. "Where's the bathroom?" he asked as he rose to his feet.

"It's the door on the left," she said. "My father dropped off your bag this morning. It's in the bathroom."

"Thanks," he mumbled, made his way to the bathroom, closed the door behind him, and groaned when he met his bloodshot eyes in the mirror. *God, I look exactly how I feel. Lovely.*

A short time later, after a long hot shower, a shave, and a couple of Tylenol, Grant began to feel human again. His nose was still slightly out of shape, but most of the swelling was gone. *Those Suttons are kicking my ass.* He was smiling when he opened the door and walked out of the bathroom.

His smile froze on his face at the sight of Viviana at the stove in jean shorts that barely covered her perfect little ass and a simple light blue tank top. She turned as she sensed his approach. "I'm making breakfast. Do you think you'll be able to keep it down?"

His cock surged to attention. *Apparently not.* "I'll try," he said and mentally added *to not suggest we skip breakfast and feed a more urgent hunger.*

How was it possible for a woman to be more beautiful each time he saw her? No makeup. No accessories. She was perfect just the way she was, with her hair swept casually up in a loose bun and her long, tan legs bare.

"Take a seat. It's almost ready."

He sat at her kitchen table. The dishes didn't match, but they were filled with an assortment of breads and pastries. He took a sip of the orange juice she'd already placed on the table. Unlike his cock, his stomach was less certain it should partake that morning. "You didn't have to go to all this trouble."

"I didn't. My brothers came by. They brought the Danishes and bagels. You were still sleeping, so I told them to come back later. They know they owe you an apology."

It was slightly mortifying to imagine her family coming and going while he was passed out on the couch, but he pushed that unappealing thought back. The only one he was upset with was himself for not being able to remember more of the night before. "I'm fine. They didn't force the drinks down me. I could have stopped at one or said no altogether."

"But you didn't know—"

He took another swig of orange juice and met her eyes. "Viv, just tell me I didn't make a complete ass of myself last night."

Her eyes rounded. "You're worried about how *you* behaved?"

"I can't believe I didn't suspect anything. I usually see a prank coming a mile away. I'm happy to admit I underestimated Dylan and Connor. They got me good."

Tears filled her eyes, and he almost knocked over the table rising to his feet. "What's wrong?"

"You're not angry."

He sat back down only because he was still feeling a little queasy. Hoping to cheer her up, he winked. "I do have three brothers. It's not my first rodeo, sweetheart."

The sweet smile she gave him was cut short by her swearing like a sailor when she realized the eggs were beginning to burn. He laughed because she was a joy on every level. Like the beer her brothers had served him, being with her packed the kind of punch no man could prepare for. All he could do was hang on and hope the ride didn't end.

Memories were slowly returning to him. He said, "Some of last night is hazy, but I do remember you announcing that I'm important to you."

She blushed as she placed a heaping plate of scrambled eggs in front of him then sat down with her own. "Do you remember telling my family you love them?"

He groaned. "No, I forgot that part."

She smiled again. "I don't think my brothers will threaten to kill you again. This morning they said they'd love to take you fishing."

"With or without a cement block tied around my ankles?" Grant joked.

She chuckled. "I didn't ask, but good point. I'll go with you if you accept."

"Oh, I accept. You'll just have to show me how to outfish them. I'm assuming there are tricks to doing it well."

"Have you ever been fishing?"

"Deep sea, yes. Once. A client of mine took me out to thank me for reorganizing his investment portfolio. I caught a 52-pound white sea bass, but I released it because it really was a striking fish. I eat fish, but I don't usually look them in the eye before I do. That one knew it, too. He gave me a good long stare that guilted me right into returning him to the water." Viviana laughed, and the happier she looked the better Grant felt.

"Connor releases them as well. Dylan teases him mercilessly about it. Once, Connor went so far as to release all their catches then buy some fillets on the way home so we could have fish for dinner. He'll be glad to have another man on his side."

"And you?" He guessed at what her answer would be, but honestly, he wasn't sure until she confirmed it.

"I catch and release. Same reason as you. I'm okay with eating animals as long as I don't meet them first."

"Hypocrites, both of us."

"Yep." She held out a plate. "Bacon?"

He took a few slices of bacon and bit into one before

adding, "Our child will probably be no better."

She froze halfway through sipping from a glass of water and started choking. When she was able to speak again, she whispered, "Our child."

He wondered if she'd said it that way because she felt as he did. Before the baby he wanted to be with her. Now, however, there was more riding on how this turned out. It was a pressure that hadn't been part of his previous relationships. He didn't consider the existence of that element good nor bad—it simply was.

He didn't share that thought, though. He was still choosing his words carefully. They were in the unique position of having their lives intimately intertwined before really knowing each other. Until that changed it was anyone's guess what the future held. "Are you hoping for a girl or a boy?" he asked.

"I'd settle for healthy," she answered without hesitation.

The fact that he would have answered his question exactly the same way brought a huge smile to his face. On the surface they could not have been more different, but in all the ways that mattered they meshed. It wasn't impossible to imagine co-parenting their child.

A knock on the door announced the arrival of her family. "Hang on," Grant called out. He finished his juice in one gulp, rose to his feet, and cracked his knuckles.

On impulse, he took Viviana by the hand and spun her in a dance move that ended with her bent over his arm in a dip his dance instructors would have applauded. While her mouth was still rounded with surprise he kissed her deeply.

He let that say what he wasn't ready to: She was his and he wasn't going anywhere.

When he released her, she looked up at him with that look again—the one that made his heart pound and his blood rush southward. "Although now I need another minute or I'm going to look really excited to see them."

Viviana laughed, a deep hearty laugh that was followed by another bang on the door. "That would be bad."

Grant imagined that scene and the problem resolved itself.

THAT NIGHT, AFTER a morning of fishing, an afternoon of touring her small hometown, and a sober dinner with her family, Grant and Viviana sat side by side on the steps of her father's house. It had been a day filled with easy laughter that had exceeded how she'd hoped Grant and her family would get along. The wonderful part was she knew it was real, her brothers would never pretend to like someone they didn't—not even for her, not even because their father told them to.

Getting to know Grant in this setting was confusing. On one hand, being with him was exciting and every look they exchanged left her glowing. On the other hand, dating while pregnant was scary as all hell. What were the rules? The pitfalls? Did she dare allow herself to imagine a traditional family unit could sprout from something that had started in a juice bar storage room?

"Are you sure you want to stay here? You could sleep on my couch again." What had seemed like an innocent suggestion came out sounding like a husky suggestion.

He flexed his shoulders and expelled a breath like a man mentally preparing himself to run a marathon. "For now, this is where I belong. It matters to your father."

"We're adults—"

He turned toward her. "Look me in the eye and tell me you don't care what your father thinks of me—of us."

She didn't even attempt that lie. "I do." She sighed. "I guess I don't know how to navigate this. What are we doing?"

He tucked her to him and kissed the top of her head. "I'm wading through an intense period of sexual frustration and determining our compatibility while facilitating a positive relationship with people I hope become my family."

"Wow, that's one way to describe it."

"What are you doing?"

Trying not to fuck you again and figuring out if a future with you is possible while hoping my family doesn't kill you. "Same as you."

He gave her a lusty grin. "Even the wading part?"

"I should say no, but, yes, even that." She slapped his shoulder playfully.

He tipped her face toward his and looked down into her eyes for a long moment. "I want you to know that when I lied to you about my last name I didn't think it would matter. I didn't think you'd matter."

Okay. Breathe. Remember he doesn't know how to phrase things well. "Should I be insulted?"

"Not at all. I'm explaining that I don't feel that way anymore. I'm saying what you said last night. You're important to me."

She caressed his cheek while gauging his level of serious-ness. Yep, he was one hundred percent not joking. *He really does need to get out of his office more and spend time with people.* "If you had left off the first part I probably would have thrown my arms around your neck, kissed you sense-less, and thought it was the most romantic thing anyone had ever said to me."

He frowned. "Which part should I have left off? About your family?"

She smiled and shook her head. "After that."

"About how you're important to me?" He looked con-fused.

She gave up, laughed, and kissed him. She'd dated men who said all the right things but didn't have half the integrity Grant did. Actions were what made a man. "Don't worry about it."

He deepened the kiss then raised his head with a smile. "You're good for me, do you know that?"

A warmth spread through her, leaving her head-to-toe happy. Taking a page from his book, she said, "I'm still deciding if you're the best thing to ever happen to me or my biggest mistake."

"Ouch," he said with a less bright smile.

She searched his face. Despite what he'd said up to this point, she needed to ask a question that kept returning to her. "Would you be here if I weren't pregnant?"

He ran gentle fingers through her hair. "Would you be with me if I weren't wealthy?"

His question floored her. "Of course I would be."

"I don't know if you knew who I was before our first meeting. I don't know if your pregnancy was an accident or strategic. If I needed you to prove your innocence, could you?"

She quickly thought of a variety of possible things she could say, but realized as she did that all would end with him having to accept her word as truth. "No, I guess I couldn't."

He traced one side of her neck. "Then the choice that lies before both of us is one of trust. I'm here with you because I want to be. If you weren't pregnant, I would still be here. You can believe me or not. There is no magic wand I can wave that will remove your doubts if you decide to hold onto them."

Had another man said the last part it might have sounded cold. The more Viviana got to know Grant the more she saw that he detached and leaned heavily on logic when things became too emotional for him. Rather than raise his voice and rant, she could imagine him organizing his point of view and hers on a spreadsheet then going over each like talking points in a meeting.

Part of her wanted to shake him and say that especially on these big life issues it was okay to be confused. Part of her wanted to hug him and ask him what had taught him to withdraw and rationalize rather than feel.

They sat there quietly for several minutes as she thought about how quickly he had become part of her life. *I said yes to dating him, but simply spending time with him isn't enough, is it, if I continue to doubt him? My fears are justifiable, but he's right—it's my choice to hold onto them or not.*

If he asked me if I'm with him for his money he must have asked himself that same question. To be honest, if I were him, those would be legitimate concerns. I did go after him. Yes, it takes two to do what we did, but a woman who wanted a rich husband might have orchestrated something like that.

And yet he is here.

Viviana said, "I called my doctor for a referral to an obstetrician. I have an appointment on Friday afternoon at two. My doctor said they'll probably do a sonogram to determine how far along I am. Would you like to come with me?"

His answer was a deep, soul shattering kiss that left her wishing they were anywhere but on her father's steps. When he ended the kiss he growled softly, "It's a date."

Could a doctor's visit be called one? Viviana's heart fluttered nervously. *So far our dates haven't exactly been conventional, so why not?* "I'll text you the information."

He nodded. "I had planned on coming back Friday night, but I'll wrap things up early." He kissed her lips softly. "I don't want to go, but I have meetings tomorrow on matters I've put off recently."

"I understand."

"I'd also like to look at the local real estate. Your apartment is nice, but I'd like our child to have a backyard to play in."

Our child. Those words never failed to send her mind scrambling to make sense of how her life had forever changed. "You don't have to—"

"I will provide for my child. That is non-negotiable," he

said with surprising steel in his voice.

Although the opposite reaction would have sickened her, she still had to ask, "And if I said no?"

The steady look he gave her sent a shiver down her spine. It brought back to mind what her father had said about Grant probably not needing a course in how to defend himself. Grant might have been patient and forgiving so far, but who was he when he wasn't? If a man with his resources turned vindictive how could she possibly protect her family from him?

"Why would you?" he finally asked.

She swallowed hard. "We may not always agree on how to raise this child. What happens then?"

"I'm sure I could bring you around to seeing reason."

She gurgled on a laugh, then realized he was serious and pulled back from him. "Or I could kick some of that arrogance out of your ass, and we could discuss it like two normal, average, ordinary parents."

"I'm not a high school boy. You don't scare me. In fact, I might enjoy that exchange." The smirk on his face told her exactly where his thoughts had gone. "And I can assure you there would be nothing average or ordinary about it."

She didn't want to laugh because it was a serious topic, but she couldn't help herself. "Or normal."

"Says the woman who still scares half the men in this town."

"Are you done?"

He shrugged, still looking far too pleased with himself. "I could be." He looked for a second as if he were waiting to see if another zinger would come to him. "Yes. That's it."

Okay, let him chew on this. "There is a house in town I'm interested in."

"Fantastic. Send me the information."

"It's three blocks from here."

"Okay."

"As in my family could walk to it."

He met her eyes without blinking. "I'm assuming the doors will have locks. Does it have a big yard? Are any homes for sale near it? We could clear an adjoining lot for a playground."

"Sure we won't need the whole block?" she suggested sarcastically.

"Would you want that much room?"

She shook her head. The way he spoke about large financial projects as if they were nothing brought home the reality of how wealthy he was. *Am I wrong to imagine he sees me as his equal?* "Sometimes you scare me."

"Because you don't know what I'll do next?"

"Yes."

He smiled.

She added, "It's not a good thing."

His smile widened. "No? On this we'll have to agree to disagree." He had that pleased with himself expression on his face again so she let the topic drop. It would have been endearing if it weren't so vital to figure him out.

Chapter Fifteen

THREE WEEKS LATER, Viviana was at her desk in her office trailer, smiling even though no one was with her. Grant said he'd end his workday early to take her to dinner. She glanced at the clock on the wall, hating it for running slower than normal that day.

She knew he'd be there at exactly five o'clock. When Grant said he would do something, he did it. When he said something mattered to him, his actions matched his words.

When her first obstetrician's appointment was moved up to two days after he'd left, she'd been apprehensive to tell him. He'd said he had a busy week ahead of him. He'd planned on seeing her around that schedule. Nevertheless, he'd said he wanted to be there for the first sonogram so she'd called him. Immediately, he'd canceled his meetings and had come back to Cairo. No questions. No hint of irritation.

When she'd asked him if he wanted to go to her first sonogram with her, she'd imagined all it would involve would be a device being run over her stomach. The ob-gyn asked them both an exhaustive number of questions then showed them a wand-like tranducer probe. She explained that the baby would be so small that this was the best way to ensure proper placement of the fetus as well as estimate the due date.

At first she was so embarrassed she couldn't look at Grant. He took her hand, though, and spoke to her gently as if he knew how vulnerable she felt. As soon as the process started, all embarrassment faded away. Grant was right there with her, squinting at the monitor screen at the hard to decipher tiny crescent shaped image the doctor assured them was their baby.

"You'll see much more on your next sonogram. I'd like to see you once a month." The doctor had turned to her computer to input information while she spoke. "Would you like to know the sex? It seems early to ask, but babies grow at remarkable speed. Your little one will be here in a blink of the eye, or at least that'll be how it feels."

Blink of the eye? I'm not ready yet. I don't have a single thing for it yet. Viviana looked to Grant as a mild panic set in. *Except him.* Grant had a similar overwhelmed expression on his face. The doctor had waved off the reaction and said, "I'll write that you're not sure, and you just tell me when you come back. How is that?"

They'd both nodded. To make herself feel better prepared, Viviana had gone out and bought several books about what to expect while expecting. The next day, stating the same reasoning, Grant had bought an office building in town.

A whole building that hadn't even been for sale. Who

does that?

Grant. Grant does that. He said he would create a satellite office here and he did.

Viviana checked the clock in her office again and her smile widened. When he'd started commuting daily from Boston to visit with her and her family she'd thought it would be too much, but the more time she spent with him the more she wanted. Never had Viviana been with a man who was as kind, considerate, or reliable as he was. As soon as she told him about her mother's foundation, a sizable anonymous donation came in that had changed the lives of several people in the community.

Add in that he was sexy as all hell and determined to get to know her before they had sex again, and what woman wouldn't have fallen a little more in love with him each day?

There was only one fly in the soup. One concern she couldn't ignore no matter how she tried to rationalize it away. The more Grant became part of her life, the less he was willing to talk about his family or friends in Boston. Whenever she brought them up, he found a way to change the subject. It was a change from when she first met him, and she didn't know what it meant, but she couldn't shake the feeling that it was important.

He knew everything about her—down to the names of her best friends in elementary school. *What do I know about him beyond who he is when he's with me?*

Is there something or someone in Boston he's running from?

Is it that his family doesn't approve of me? Are they rejecting our child?

She pushed that thought back because it had the power to sour her otherwise great mood. *There's nothing to worry about. We don't have to rush. While waiting for our little one to arrive, we have plenty of time to figure each other out.*

AT EXACTLY FIVE o'clock Grant stepped into Viviana's office and swung her up in his arms. He lacked the words to describe how good it felt to return to her. One day soon he intended to end each night loving her and wake each morning to her snuggled to his side. "Hey, beautiful, you ready to go?"

She kissed him boldly and soundly.

He ended the kiss with a regretful chuckle and a mental reminder to his hardening cock that fasting now would be rewarded with a lifetime of feasting. It remained defiantly overeager.

Viviana had offered her couch to Grant again, and despite his frustration, he'd declined a second time. There was an order to things and a reason for that order.

He wasn't going to marry a woman he didn't know.

He couldn't truly know Viviana unless he expanded their relationship beyond how much he wanted to fuck her again. None of his initial concerns had anything to do with their sexual compatibility. No, that box had been the first one checked off.

However, he'd also wanted to see her with her family.

With her friends.

When she was happy, angry, sad.

He wasn't a short-term investor. Once he committed it

would be for life. Over the last few weeks she'd exceeded his expectations and surprised him again and again.

He'd expected to be amused by her, but she could tell a story even better than her brothers. He'd never laughed as much as he had with her.

He knew she was good with people, but he hadn't realized how good until he'd seen her in action. Watching her crack the whip then offer carrots of encouragement gave him a whole new respect for how smoothly her father's company ran. Small problems didn't have time to grow into larger ones because she nipped them in the bud. He understood now why she was both adored and respected by the workers. It wasn't out of deference to her father or brothers. If an argument ensued between two of the crew, she marched out of her office to address it. She could intimidate men twice her size then leave them smiling and smitten when she walked away. He wished his executive staff had half her team management skills.

Grant had never considered himself a people person, but he could listen to her for hours and walk away wishing they'd had more time. His original plan had been to work in the city all week and see Viviana only on the weekends. Being invited back early to attend her first sonogram had been such a relief that he'd given up on the idea of taking things slowly with her. Sometimes even the most careful planner had to leap when his instincts told him to.

As predictable as a sunrise? Not anymore.

I don't want to go back to that life. I want this—with her.

"I have a surprise for you," he murmured. "A present."

"You didn't have to get me anything," she said as she checked his hands to see if he was holding anything.

"I know, but I wanted to." He laughed at the child-like excitement in her eyes.

"Do you have it on you?"

"No."

"Give me a hint. Living or non-living?"

"I'm not saying. How will it be a surprise if you guess what it is?"

"My family never did surprises. Come on, just a little hint." She ran her hands up the front of his jacket, but he caught them with his before they reached his breast pocket. Although it wasn't what he was referring to, he didn't want her to feel the ring box.

"Let's go. We don't want to be late. It's my turn to cook."

She laughed. "You mean *your private chef's* turn."

He kissed her on the tip of her nose. "Your family says it counts."

"It's cheating." Her eyes were dancing with the delight of teasing him.

"So is ordering pizza, but we eat it every fifth night."

Her mouth opened and shut without a word coming out. When a little line appeared between her eyebrows he knew he'd won. "Okay, cough up the surprise. I can't take it anymore."

He shook his head and smiled. "Not yet. Grab your purse. I can't be late."

She did, then linked hands with him as they exited the

trailer together. "You should give me three chances to guess it."

He pretended to consider it. "In exchange for what?"

Instantly her cheeks reddened and her voice turned breathless. "What would you want?"

Images of her on her knees taking him deeply in her mouth flashed through his mind, but he shoved them back. Just as quick, his accommodating psyche recreated vivid images of how she'd clung to him as he'd pounded into her. He nearly changed his mind and dragged her back into the trailer, but he'd put a lot of effort into making sure the evening would go smoothly.

He had the ring.

He'd invited her family.

They knew where and at what time to meet them.

All that was left was to give her the surprise, give her the ring, and set a date.

He opened the passenger side of his car and picked a folder off the seat. He took it with him after closing her door and walking around to his. Once inside, he tapped the folder on the steering wheel a few times as he considered showing her the contents. "I also have something for your family, but I'm not one hundred percent certain they'll like it."

Perhaps it was the seriousness of his tone that brought the look of concern to her eyes. "Do you want me to look at it first?"

Although he appreciated her offer, he tucked the folder on the side of his seat and shook his head. Yes, Viviana had added light and color to his life, but he didn't want to have the same relationship with her family that he had with his. He wanted to be as real with them as he was with her.

Being himself was something he had never comfortably done in Boston. Here, he didn't have to be perfect. Things made sense, and people said what they thought. It wasn't the emotional minefield he was tired of navigating with his own family. At first he'd felt guilty about answering his siblings' phone calls with brief texts, but giving himself time away from them was freeing.

With Viviana and her family he'd found what he hadn't known he'd craved—a place where he could be himself. He was excited to finally have a tangible way of showing them what they meant to him.

Go big or go home.

Chapter Sixteen

VIVIANA WAS CONFUSED when they drove past her father's home and kept going. She almost said something, but Grant was obviously taking her somewhere else, and wherever it was he couldn't hide his excitement about it. He glanced at her several times, each time his smile growing wider.

"You have no idea where we're going, do you?"

"I don't."

"I'm impressed with your family's ability to keep a secret."

"What did you bribe them with?"

"I may have promised to lend your brothers my Spider." They pulled over to the side of the road. "But I couldn't have finished without their help." He stopped, then added, "Actually, I could have, but it wouldn't have been as much fun."

His smile was so bright, so mesmerizing, that rather than look around she simply smiled back at him. She was more excited by the idea that he'd spent time planning something with her family than she could possibly be over wherever they were going. "You're crazy if you let my brothers drive so much as your lawnmower."

"I don't own one of those. At least, I don't think I do."

"Uh huh. Well, after my brothers are done with your car, you may not own a Spider either."

"Viv?"

"Yes?"

"Stop talking and look behind you."

She turned in her seat and looked out her window. The front of the house she'd told him she was interested in buying was freshly painted, and its yard was beautifully landscaped. What caught and held her attention, though, was her father and brothers sitting on the porch waving at her. "What are they doing there?" The answer came to her in a whoosh. "Did you buy the house?"

"No, you and I did. We bought the houses around it, too, but I thought it'd be too obvious if I started demolishing them. It was hard enough to renovate the inside without you noticing."

"You renovated the inside? In a couple of weeks? That's impossible."

He shrugged. "It's funny what becomes possible if you throw enough money at it."

She was happy and scared in equal amounts. "That's a fast renovation." *And a fast step in our relationship. One I'm not sure I'm ready for.*

He took her hand in his. "I want to live with you in that house. I want to raise our children there."

"Children? We're only having one."

"I'm sure we'll want more. I come from a large family. You're one of three. Money's not a problem for us so we could have a dozen if we wanted."

"A dozen?" Her head started to spin as panic rose within her. "That sounds—" *Frightening. Exhausting. Crazy.*

"Wonderful, doesn't it?" he finished for her.

"Actually—"

"Viviana Sutton"—he took a box out of his breast pocket and flipped it open, revealing a huge diamond solitaire— "will you—?"

"Let's take a minute to think about this first." She snapped the box shut. *Oh, my God. Oh. My. God.*

He gave her a long look then slowly opened the box again. "It's an engagement ring," he said, as if there was a possibility she'd confused it with something else. "The last three weeks have been amazing. We fit. We enjoy each other. Marry me. We'll make us official and our baby will be a Barrington."

Reason battled with euphoria. The diamond dwarfed any she'd seen in person and flashed like a lit-up stop sign. "This is so fast."

"The best way to miss an opportunity is to hesitate instead of acting."

She hugged herself and glanced again at her family on the porch of the home he'd bought for her. It would be so easy to say yes, but if they made a mistake now, it wasn't just them who would pay the price. "I don't know. I need to think this through."

"What is there to think through? Name the obstacle and

I'll remove it."

With her heart thudding wildly, she searched his face. He was sincere. *But*— "What does your family think of us getting engaged?"

His expression closed. "They'll be fine with it."

"Will be. You haven't told them?"

He shrugged.

She looked from him to her family and back to him. "But you told mine?"

He nodded. "I asked them for their blessing, yes."

From the big smiles on her brothers' faces, she knew they expected her to leave the car with a ring on her finger. Her gaze flew back to Grant. *Is this all so the baby can be a Barrington?* He bought an office building so he could work from here. He bought a house for us. He didn't have to do that. *Am I crazy to worry?*

I'm falling for him, but how can I give him my heart when he is giving me only half of himself? Audrey would probably slap me senseless for hesitating, but isn't this the best time to ask my questions? If we can't talk to each other now, what kind of marriage would we have? "Do you love me?" she asked softly.

He opened his mouth to say something then snapped his teeth together and said nothing. In one way it was a letdown, in another it supported her instincts. "No one would ever take better care of you than I will. You and our baby will never want for anything." He kissed her then and her willpower nearly crumbled.

She broke the kiss off and framed his face with her hands. "Promise me something."

"Anything," he answered huskily.

"Promise you won't ask again until your answer is yes."

"I—I—Okay."

She fell even more in love with him because he could have lied, but they'd sworn to be honest with each other. "And I want to meet your family."

His expression tightened. "Why?"

"Because they're a part of you." She took a deep breath and plowed on. "I'm falling for you, but I can't love half a man. I don't know if you're ashamed of me or what we did, but—"

"I'm not." His expression turned pained. "God, don't even think that. Meeting you has been like being given a second chance at life."

"What was wrong with your first chance?"

She sensed him withdrawing mentally before he withdrew physically. He pocketed the ring box and sat back in his seat. His hand grazed the top of the folder he'd brought with him. He picked it up and held it up between them as if it contained the answers to her questions. "I'm not half a man here. I'm the man I've always wanted to be."

"I don't understand. Help me understand."

GRANT DIDN'T KNOW how to explain it since it was something he was still figuring out. He'd never been comfortable talking about his emotions and growing up sharing them was discouraged. In the Barrington home, all that had mattered was how things appeared. Yes, things were changing, but to an extreme he didn't know how to deal with.

How could he take Viviana into that mess?

"Tell me about your family," she ordered softly.

"I have."

"I know their names. I know what they do for a living. I don't know what kind of people they are. Do you get along with them? Did they do something that makes you want to hide here with me?"

"I'm not hiding." His neck warmed as his pride took a hit. *Is that how she sees me?* It stung that she might have the same view of him as his family did.

"Then talk to me."

He looked out the window at her family who was still watching them. "This is going nowhere. Let's go eat."

She touched his forearm, bringing his attention back to her. "You just asked me to marry you. You want to live with me, raise a child with me. How can we do that if you won't let me in?"

"What do you want from me?"

"The truth."

His phone beeped with a message. He checked the caller ID. It was Ian. Something in him snapped and he growled, "We all think we want the truth, but it doesn't make anything better. In fact, sometimes the truth has the power to destroy everyone you care about and drag you down as well. I thought I was doing the right thing. I might have had a moment or two when I imagined I could fix what was wrong with my family. I saw myself as some kind of fucking unsung hero who'd just been given a chance to prove himself. I didn't help my family. I handed them a loaded gun. Judge me if you must, but I can't stomach watching my family fall apart a second time. That's why you haven't met them."

Viviana took his hand and brought it up to her face. "Whatever happened, Grant, I know you're a good man. I needed time away from family to find a way back to them. Maybe it's the same for you."

"I wish it were that simple. It's more fucked up than that."

"Okay. Just know I'm here when you're ready to tell me." He thought she would push him for more, but she didn't. She simply sat there, holding his hand against her cheek and smiling at him with her heart in her eyes. So beautiful, he could barely breathe.

I should have said I love her, but what the hell do I know about love?

His phone beeped again. He didn't check it this time. Whatever his family was so urgently trying to tell him could wait until after dinner. Despite what she'd said, he didn't want to expose her to . . .

Oh, my God, this is what my father did with my mother. He was so afraid she might have another breakdown, he maintained a distance between her and anything unpleasant. We children came second to his need to shelter her.

I'm recreating that with Viviana. Is that what I want? A family based on an illusion of perfection? Viviana is not my mother. She's strong. She doesn't want the fairy tale.

The look in her eyes told him everything he needed to know. *She wants me. The real me. And she's not going to settle for less.*

He brought her hand to his mouth and kissed her knuckles. "How was I lucky enough to find you?"

She grinned. "I believe I found you."

"Oh, yes," memories of that first day came rushing back and he was suddenly turned on as well as confused, and that never helped a man sort his thoughts out.

The color that rose in her cheeks meant she was getting good at reading his thoughts. He glanced down at the bulge in the front of his jeans. *So subtle.*

He kissed her gently then sat back even though he craved more. Her family was expecting to celebrate an engagement, not a public mauling. He glanced over his shoulder. Dylan had a plate in one hand. He shamelessly shoveled a bite of food into his mouth then waved the fork in the air to summon them. Connor tapped his watch. Her father stood with his arms folded across his chest, watching.

"This is going to be awkward," Grant said.

She raised a finger in the air toward her family as a sign that they needed another moment. When she looked back at Grant, her eyes were troubled. "I'm sorry."

He pulled her into his arms. "Don't be. I always know how I stand with you, and you have no idea how much I value that." He kissed her again. "I will ask again."

She kissed him back. "You'd better."

His phone rang another time, and he groaned. He held the phone up and said, "I have an idea about why my family is calling, but it could be anything at this point. I can try to prepare you, or I can let you dive in and hear it for yourself."

She studied his face for a moment. "Either way as long as

you're okay to share it. It's okay if you're not. I understand now."

He took a deep, fortifying breath and made his decision. She'd been a playmate and a friend. Marrying her was something he'd decided made sense because of how well they got along, both in and out of bed. But this—this was deeper. She was offering him the kind of loving acceptance he'd stopped believing was possible. It shook him to the core. He wished he could go back to the first moment they met and do everything that followed better.

I can't imagine my life without her in it.

Is that love?

"I—I—" His phone went to voicemail then started ringing again. "I'm ready." He answered and pressed speakerphone. "Ian, sorry, I was in the middle of something. What do you need?"

"You need to get your ass home," Ian barked. "I can't contain this on my own. I'm doing everything I can to keep it out of the news. I can only call in so many favors. I know you asked for time to sort out your own shit, but you need to know what's going on because it's spiraling out of control."

Viviana's mouth rounded in surprise.

"Ready?" he mouthed silently.

Viviana nodded.

Grant asked aloud, "What's going on?"

"Yesterday, at the family meeting you were too busy to attend, Mom and Dad announced the results of the DNA testing. The baby they buried wasn't Kent."

"What?" Grant asked in shock.

"You heard me right. They don't know who that baby was, but it wasn't related to us. Mom is convinced that means Kent is alive and out there. Emily is the only reason Asher hasn't gone after Stiles again, but I don't know how much longer he's going to listen to her. He wants to beat the truth out of Stiles. Helene's parents flew in when they heard the news. She and Andrew are in hiding with them. They're not answering my calls, so I don't know what they're up to. Kenzi and Mom tried to hire that woman, Alethea Niacharos, but she said she's waiting to hear from you. I was going to talk to her myself, but didn't you fire her because her methods were illegal?" Without giving Grant time to answer, Ian continued, "Oh, and did I mention that Dax conveniently disappeared on a business trip with Lance. Seriously? Lance? Who do they think they're fooling? Your guess is as good as mine on which member of our family is going to get arrested or killed first. You need to get back here and help me talk some sense into everyone."

Grant let out a long breath. "Viviana, this is my brother, Ian. Ian, you're on speakerphone with Viviana Sutton."

"What is wrong with you? Get me off speakerphone. Now."

"No." Grant laced his fingers with Viviana's and held on for the ride. "I trust Viviana."

Viviana smiled gently.

"Has everyone lost their minds?" Ian growled. "This is a nightmare."

"Can I call you back, Ian?"

"You're joking, right?"

"I'm not. I'll come home, but there's something I need to do first."

"You know what? I don't care. Come home or don't. At this point I don't know if you'd be any help anyway. You brought this on us."

"Me?" Grant asked between gritted teeth.

"I knew telling Mom was a bad idea. What will be your next gift to her? Another baby's body to bury? A movie deal where this can all play out for public entertainment?"

Viviana blanched, but Grant wasn't angered by Ian's attack. He could have reminded his brother he had agreed their mother deserved to know the truth, but it wouldn't have helped the situation. Of all his brothers, Ian was the most like Grant. He was a rational problem solver who didn't panic. If Ian thought the situation was out of control, it was. If he was worried, there was reason to be. "I'll call you in a few."

Ian hung up without saying another word.

For a long moment Grant and Viviana simply sat there looking at each other. It was difficult to guess what she was thinking. Grant had difficulty imagining what he would have thought had their situations been reversed.

"Who is Stiles?" she asked.

"Helene's uncle."

"Your brother's fiancée?"

"Andrew, yes."

"Why does Asher think he knows anything?"

She was handling the story much more calmly than he'd expected. "Stiles owned the clinic my brother died at. He claims he was paid to cover up that my deceased aunt paid to have Kent killed."

Viviana nodded slowly.

"You're taking this well."

Viviana's eyes rounded. "Oh, I'm freaking out on the inside. It's heartbreaking and a lot to take in."

"For me as well."

"So, when do we go to Boston?"

His jaw went slack. "You can't still want to meet my family." He searched her face for a sign of revulsion or fear but found none.

"Mine almost gave you alcohol poisoning, and you're still here."

"We're quite the pair." He laughed even though his gut was still twisted and anxious. *Am I insane to consider taking her back with me?*

"Do you mind if I ask you a few questions?"

He didn't and spent the next ten or so minutes clarifying who everyone was and how his family had gotten to this place. When he finished, she asked for a moment to think. He wouldn't have blamed her if what she was pondering was how the hell to get out of meeting his crazy family. He wouldn't tell her she couldn't go, though. He wasn't going to close a door on her.

Her stomach made a rumbling sound. "Can you make phone calls from your helicopter? If so, I'd call Asher and tell him we're on our way. I bet that will keep him in Boston. Then you should call that woman—Alethea? Unless you still don't want to work with her, but if not, you should suggest someone else to your mother. I wouldn't call Ian until you know where Lance and Dax went, but they probably have their phones with them so that's just another phone call. Then it's really a matter of finding out what happened to your brother, but you sound like you're good at stuff like that."

"I am," Grant said with a bemused smile. She was tackling his family's disaster with the ease that he'd seen her tackle issues with the construction crew. More amazing? He agreed with her plan. Except possibly that last part. This wasn't a scheduling mistake with machinery. "Alethea probably does know something, but my aunt was a sociopath. If she switched the babies, do we really want to know what she did with the one she took? It might be even more heinous." He laid his head back and closed his eyes. "Ian had a point. I brought this on my family. I didn't have to tell my mother what I'd discovered."

"Fuck Ian," Viviana said harshly.

Grant's head snapped up, and his eyes flew open.

Viviana continued, "You did what you thought was right. Your mother was lied to for too long. She deserved the truth. And she deserves to know if Kent is still alive. You could give her that closure." She took his hand and laid it on her stomach. "If it were our child, I wouldn't be able to rest until I knew the truth, and I would want to know every last detail, no matter how bad it was. And if there were even the tiniest chance that he was still alive? Nothing could stop me from looking for him. Nothing."

Suddenly, what had seemed like a muddled mess to him

was crystal clear. When he imagined his child disappearing and not knowing if it was alive or dead, he knew Ian was wrong. *My mother needs the truth, and I'm going to find it for her.* He pulled her to him for another hug. "Thank you, Viviana." Emotions swirled through Grant, and his heart felt like it might burst from his chest. He struggled to find the words to express what he felt for Viviana so he kissed her instead, deeply, tenderly.

A knock on the window made them both jump. Dylan and Connor were at the driver's side with plates of food. Grant lowered the window.

Dylan handed bundled silverware along with a plate of steak and potatoes through the window. "You guys are getting too hot and heavy for me to keep taking photos. I thought you might want memories of when you proposed, but it's getting weird." He flipped to a photo of the two of them facing each other. "This one looked promising." Then there was one of them kissing. He deleted it. "I thought I saw a ring in this one." He flipped to another. "Then you looked like you were arguing so I stopped. I took a beer break and then it looked like you might be asking her again. Honestly, Dad is ready to go home, so if you haven't said yes yet could you hurry it along or call us later with the news?" He chucked Grant on the shoulder. "Nice house, though. It came out good."

Connor bent down. "So, where's the ring?"

I'll just get it out there. "She said no."

"You said no?" Connor asked, his mouth flopping open. "Oh, man, that sucks, Grant. Sorry."

Dylan started deleting more photos. "You're not going to want these then."

Connor looked at the plate in his hand. "Viv, you're probably too upset to eat, right?"

Viviana leaned over Grant and made a grab for the plate. "Don't you dare touch my steak, Connor. Hand it over."

Looking disappointed, Connor did. "It was delicious. How much does a private chef cost? We should get one of our own."

Grant snapped his fingers and reached for the folder he'd prepared for them. He handed it to Connor. "This might help with that."

"What is it?" Dylan asked as he swiped it.

"It's for your father. Just a few ideas on how he could restructure his business health plan, claim more deductions, invest those savings in low-risk stocks to provide a better retirement program for his employees, and in general minimize his profit loss."

Dylan shrugged and handed it back to his brother. "Oh. I'll let Connor go over it with him. I find that stuff boring."

Connor made a face. "Fine, but then you have to tell Dad that Viviana turned Grant down. She probably would have said yes if you hadn't made it into a photo shoot."

Dylan glared at Connor. "This isn't my fault."

"I'm not saying it is. I'm just saying it might be," Connor said with a shrug.

"You're an idiot," Dylan said.

Connor held up his hands and mimed taking photos. "I would have stopped when they kissed the first time, but that's me."

With a growl, Dylan punched Connor in the arm. "Shut the fuck up. I didn't know they'd go all porno with Dad there."

"Poor Grant." Connor shook his head. "He's taking it better than I would."

Dylan shrugged and the two started to walk away. "And he's still mooning over her. Men are stupid when they're in love. Have some pride, dude."

Viviana covered her face with one hand and groaned. "I'm so sorry."

"Don't be. They're always like watching a sitcom." *Besides, I am stupid because I do love you. I love you.* "Viv, I—"

She held up a hand to halt him from saying more. "I don't want to face my father yet, either. I'll text him that I'm okay and we're heading up to meet your family. That'll make sense to him and it's true." She popped a potato wedge in her mouth. "I'll explain everything to him later, but first let's find Kent."

Okay. First we find Kent, then I propose again, the right way.

Chapter Seventeen

A WEEK LATER, while in flight across the Pacific Ocean to Bright, Australia, Viviana was naked and curled up against Grant's side on the bed of his private jet. She'd never flown on anything so extravagant and had been nervous at first. However, after having sex against the hallway leading out of the main cabin, then in the shower, and one last leisurely time on the bed, she was feeling quite relaxed. She traced the strong muscles of his chest and said, "If this flight is much longer I'll need a day of rest before going to see Mrs. Thompson."

He nuzzled her neck. "I missed you. I missed this side of us."

"Apparently." She chuckled. "Me, too."

He ran a gentle hand down her neck, across her collarbone, and down her arm. "Have I told you how amazing you are?"

"You may have mentioned it once or twice, but don't let that stop you."

"My parents adore you, just as I knew they would. Kenzi told me the women in the family think you're exactly what I need. Lance almost pissed himself when Asher refused to arm wrestle you; he thinks Asher was afraid to lose. Even Ian calmed down after meeting you. You not only helped me pull my family back from the brink of chaos, but you won them over while doing it. That is no small achievement."

Her face warmed with a pleased blush. "You told me to be myself around them so I was."

He kissed her nose. "Maybe just a tad less swearing in front of my dad, though."

"I'll try. You know how I get when I'm nervous," she said with a grimace.

Grant shrugged and smiled. "On second thought, it's probably good for him. He needs to lighten up." He tucked a hair behind her ear. "I didn't tell any of them we're going to Australia."

"Are you feeling guilty?" She raised herself up on one elbow, not minding at all that his attention was instantly drawn to the jiggle of her bare breasts. She loved that he found pleasure in her body because she certainly found pleasure in his. Despite being sated from their sexual marathon, she ran her hand down his stomach and loved that his cock surged in her hand.

He closed his eyes and groaned with pleasure. "I'm trying to have a serious conversation with you but it's hard—because I am again—that's what you do to me. You reduce me to a bumbling, horny mess."

"Sorry." She moved her hand away from his sex. Their attraction to each other was addictive, but there was a serious reason for their trip. "What were you saying?"

He opened his eyes. "I forget. It was important though."

Viviana pulled the bedsheet up to her chin. "Should I cover the distraction?"

"No, but this might help." He bunched up a piece of the sheet and pretended to stuff it in her mouth.

She swatted his hand away. "Oh, you'll pay for that."

He laughed, rolled onto his back and pulled her onto him so she was straddling him. "I certainly hope so."

Looking down at him, laughing with him like she was, she knew she would never love another the way she loved him. They were two people who shouldn't complement each other, yet somehow they did on a level neither had experienced before. Sometimes the intensity of their connection scared her, but she refused to let that ruin her time with him. "All joking aside, what did you want to say?"

He rested his hands on her bare hips. "I have a feeling Alethea's instincts about Pamela Thompson are right. Her brother was a custodian at Stiles's clinic. She was a nurse there. Her brother drowned in a pool at a hotel he wasn't staying at. It had to be murder. Pamela fled without telling anyone where she was going or taking any of her things with her. People do that when they're afraid. She might be another dead end, but there's a good chance she knows what happened to Kent. Tomorrow morning we could be heading home in an entirely different mood."

She didn't know what Grant was about to say, but she'd learned to give him time to find his words. Meeting his family had shown her why he'd built such a large buffer zone between them and his emotions. He'd never stopped caring about them, but he'd learned to protect himself by hiding in his work.

What was truly beautiful about him was that even as he'd pulled away, he never stopped taking care of his family. She'd listened to the teasing stories his siblings had shared and the common thread she'd heard was that nothing—not mockery, not rejection—stopped him from doing what he knew was best for his family. In her eyes, he was already the hero he thought he'd failed to become.

No, not the chest pounding, strutting type his family seemed to admire. Grant chose a quieter path. It was one with less fanfare and gratitude, but more noble in its goal because it served the greater good rather than his ego.

She'd once considered him weak because he took a punch without striking back. Now that she knew him she understood he was strong enough to not need to win every fight. One day, she hoped his family would see him for the remarkable man he was. Finding Kent could be what would finally open their eyes.

"Are you paying attention?" he asked with a smile.

"Sorry," she said, returning her attention to him. "I was thinking about how wonderful you are."

His eyes narrowed playfully. "Good cover story. Now focus. This is important."

"Yes, sir."

He opened a drawer beside the bed and took out the ring box she'd once rejected. "You set a criteria for me proposing again that I can now meet. Viviana Sutton, I love you. No one has ever stood by me the way you have. You inspire me to be bolder. You humble me by refocusing me on what is most important in life—family. Marry me because there is no me without you—no me I want to be."

With tears filling her eyes she leaned down and kissed him. She could have simply said yes, but what would have been the fun in that? She raised her head and asked, "Even if I'm ordinary and average?"

There was a time when he would have rushed to deny it, and she would have doubted his explanation, but they were past that. A cocky grin spread across his face. "Even then."

She pinched his side, but not too hard. With him, she was also strong enough to not need the win. They were on the same side. "Let me see that ring again," she asked as if she weren't bursting with happiness over his proposal.

He took it out of the box and held it before her. At the same time, she edged back onto him so his hardening cock was enfolded by her sex. She began to move her hips back and forth, wetting him while exciting herself. "I'll have to think about this before deciding this time."

"Think hard," he growled and pulled back, thrusting himself deeply inside her. "And fast."

She gasped with pleasure and her movements became more circular. There was no rush, just a slow, steady burn. "It's the right size. Not too big. Not too small."

He thrust upward again. "I'm glad you like it. Now say yes and give me your fucking finger."

She bent over him, plundering his mouth thoroughly, before whispering against his lips, "Yes."

He'd dropped the ring during their kiss and had to feel

around on the bed beside him for it. All the while, she used her hips to take him deeper and her inner muscles to tighten around him. By the time he slid the ring on her finger, they were both glistening with sweat and hungry to taste more of each other.

He rolled them so he was above and kissed her breasts gently before thrusting harder and faster into her. The ring sparkled on the hand she ran across his powerful shoulders, adding another layer to this claiming.

She was his, body, mind, and soul.

He was hers just as completely.

Sex was now as much about joining up as it was about the pleasure. She wanted him closer, deeper, in her mouth, all around her. He was every breath she took and when she finally gave herself over to an orgasm it was like slow moving lava that overtook her inch by inch until it consumed her.

He groaned as he came then growled, "Mine," in her ear.

She tightened her legs around him in a full body hug and growled back, "Always."

Chapter Eighteen

As Grant parked his rental car on the street beneath a large maple tree, he glanced into the rearview mirror in time to spot another car pull onto a side street. He scanned the area in front of the car and nodded when he saw a brunette jogging toward them. Marc and Alethea were not as stealthy as they liked to believe, not if one paid attention to their patterns of behavior. Confirming their presence lessened Grant's concern about bringing Viviana with him. He wanted her to be part of this, but he didn't want to put her in danger, and no one knew what Pamela Thompson's reaction would be to their questions.

"My father just texted me. He said you're a genius and thank you," Viviana said. "He also said next time don't give anything that important to Dylan and Connor. They forgot to give the folder to him. He found it in the living room when he went back to check on our house."

Grant laughed. "I was wondering why he hadn't said anything."

She leaned over and kissed him on the cheek. "Thank you for taking care of my family in a way that leaves them with their pride. It would have been easy for you to throw money at them, but they would have felt you thought you were better than them. My dad says you're a keeper, and he's never liked anyone I've dated."

Grant's heart pounded. *She understands.*

"So, are we doing good cop/bad cop?" she asked quickly in an excited tone. "Can I be the bad cop?"

With her expertise with colorful expletives, he was sure she could nail that role, but he preferred a more subtle approach. "She's not a criminal, at least not as far as we know. She may have feared for her life when she fled. We can't scare her. I don't want to chance her running again before we know what she knows."

"Gotcha. Good cop/good cop."

"Or no cop. We're just people asking questions."

Hand in hand they walked up onto the wrap-around porch of a small brick home. It was nicely kept, but modest. Grant knocked on the door.

Barking ensued, followed by a woman hushing them and telling one to lie down. A moment later, a flustered brunette with a wild amount of curls and a bright smile opened the door. She looked about the age Pamela Thompson was said to be: 55. "You're early," she said in a rush, "but I'm glad you brought your husband. Wait until you see them. It breaks my heart to part with them, but I didn't even want one dog—I certainly can't have five."

"No, of course not," Viviana said smoothly. "We've been shopping around and talking to so many people lately that everyone's stories have blended into one in my head. Where did they come from again?"

And just like that, Pamela led them into the house and invited them to have a seat on her couch. A black, long-haired female retriever ambled over to them and laid her head on Grant's knee. He petted it absently and let Viviana take the lead.

"It's a long story. Would you like a glass of water?"

Both Viviana and Grant said they would. Once they were all seated in the living room, the woman said, "Opal is a flat-coated retriever. She came to me when my neighbors decided to move closer to their grandchildren. They didn't tell me she was pregnant so I don't know who the father was, but if you're willing to take a chance on them, I can't imagine sweeter puppies. She's a love, and I'm sure they will be, too. Would you each like to hold one?"

"That's not—" Grant started to say.

"We would love to," Viviana spoke over him.

The woman returned with two squirming black puppies. One was all black, the other had a stripe of white down its nose and belly. She handed one to each of them. Grant's only experience with dogs had been Kenzi's rescue. He wasn't prepared for the amount of slobber and kisses that one small animal could deliver. He would have put it down, but at least to start with, it was important to appear interested. "This is a lively one," he tried to sound pleased.

Viviana was cuddling hers, and it looked ready to fall asleep. *Sure, she gets the quiet one.*

"So, have you lived in Bright long? We're in an apartment now, but we're looking to buy a home," Grant said.

The woman looked concerned. "I've been here almost thirty years. Make sure a puppy is okay with your landlord before you decide on one. I'd hate for you to have to bring it back." She smiled as if reminiscing. "Everything changes once you take them home and fall in love with them."

"Oh, we've already cleared it with the landlord."

"That's good," the woman said with relief.

"Thirty years," Grant said, "and yet I hear a slight accent. You're not native to Australia, are you? Where were you originally from?"

The woman's smile faded. "So, the female is the runt of the litter and the one your husband is holding should be one of the largest. If you're looking for an active dog, I'd choose the male. If you want one that will lie at your feet, I'd choose the female."

Grant exchanged a look with Viviana and made a decision. "We're not actually here about the puppies."

The woman's eyes widened and she stood. "Then what are you here for?"

Viviana continued to cuddle the puppy to her. "We're hoping you could help us find someone or find out what happened to him."

The woman clasped her hands in front of her. "I'm always willing to help out when I can. Who are you looking for?"

Grant put the squirming puppy down by his feet. "You are Pamela Thompson, yes?"

"That's right."

"Was your maiden name Thorsen?"

She shook her head. "What is this about? Who are you?"

Grant stood. "We know most of the story already, we're looking for you to fill in what we don't. You can either talk to us or the authorities we'll send here. One way or another, we'll get the answers we came for."

Pale, and with shaking hands, the woman picked up the puppy and returned it to a small pen then held out her hands to take the puppy back from Viviana. "I have no idea what you think I might know, but you should go now."

Viviana handed her the puppy, but held onto it a moment after the woman accepted it. "No one thinks you were involved. We think you might have seen or heard something. That's all. We don't want to disrupt your life here or put you in any danger, but if you know something . . . please."

The woman placed the second puppy back in the pen and walked to the door. "I have no idea what you're talking about, but I will call the police if you don't leave now."

"Would you? Would you risk it? I don't think so," Grant said in a low tone.

Viviana tugged on his arm and shook her head. "She's scared. That won't work," she whispered.

"Get out of my house—now," the woman said as she reached for her phone. "Or I most certainly will have you arrested for trespassing." She paused then said, "I wish I could help you, but I can't. Sorry."

Viviana frowned then said, "Grant, can I see your phone?"

He handed it to her without hesitation.

Viviana flipped through his photos until she came across

a photo of his family. She held it out so the woman could see it. "We're not the only ones looking for this person. Do you see the parents in this photo? They were told their son died during childbirth thirty years ago at a clinic in Aruba where you and your brother worked. Sophie Barrington has mourned the loss of that son for thirty years, but she just found out the baby she buried wasn't hers. Can you imagine how that is tearing her apart? The guilt? Worse—the hope that he might still be alive somewhere. She never forgot him. None of his siblings ever forgot him." She touched Grant's arm. "All Grant wants is to find out what happened to his brother so he can give his mother the comfort of the truth—the peace that one only finds in closure. You're our only lead, our only hope of finding out what happened to Kent Barrington."

A large older man walked into the room. "So are you taking one puppy or three?" he joked. When the room remained silent and still all humor left his face. "Pam, is everything okay?"

Pam raised a shaking hand to her mouth. "No."

The man moved to stand protectively in front of Pamela. "I don't know what's going on here, but either start explaining or get the hell out of my house."

Pamela covered her stomach with her other arm as if she were about to get sick. Grant watched both expressions carefully. *She doesn't want him to know what we're doing here.*

He doesn't know.

Grant guessed at their relationship and followed his instincts on how to salvage a chance to speak to Pamela more.

"We were undecided if we wanted a dog from a shelter, and my fiancée may have accidently offended your wife by saying she doesn't approve of private breeders. I'm sure it's the kind of misunderstanding we can put behind us. We know now that your wife has what we're looking for."

Pamela shook her head. "I don't. Please, just go."

Grant squared his shoulders. "Even if we leave now, we'll be back."

"I don't like the way you're talking to my wife," the man said, rising to his full height.

"Please," Viviana said, flipping to another photo. "This is Kenzi Barrington. She's happily married, but she is plagued by questions about what happened to her twin. She believes he's still alive. Imagine her pain. Anything you know could help ease it. Even if it's something so horrible you don't want to remember, please remember just this one last time so she can finally have her answers."

Pamela kept hugging herself and shaking her head. Her husband put his arm around her. "What is this about, Pam? What are they talking about?"

"I think it has something to do with Neil, but I don't know anything. He ran with a tough crowd. Maybe he got mixed up in something, but he wouldn't have told me about it."

The man nodded and hugged his wife. "She's telling you the truth. Her brother was a gambler, and when he owed money he didn't care how he got it. Eventually that got him killed. It's not something we like to talk about, but if he somehow hurt someone you knew, all we can offer you is our sympathy. You'll never meet a more soft-hearted woman than my wife. If she knew anything, if she thought she could help you, she would."

Disappointment swept through Grant. Her brother might have known something, but he was dead. She didn't seem to know anything. This was another dead end.

VIVIANA SAW GRANT'S shoulders slump, but she wasn't ready to give up yet. Pamela's reaction was too strong, too scared. She had to know something so horrible she had never even told her husband—something she wanted to keep a secret from him even thirty years later. What would keep a thirty-year-old crime that fresh? "You know where he is, don't you, Pamela? He's not dead, is he? Kent Barrington is alive."

Tears filled Pamela's eyes.

"What is she talking about, Pam? I know everyone you know, and we don't know any Barringtons."

A tear slid down Pamela's cheek. "Could I see those photos?" she asked.

Viviana handed her the phone.

Pamela swiped through the family album. "My brother never told me his name. He came to my house after the deed was done. There was nothing I could do. Neil said anyone who knew anything was in danger. He told me to hide, and if he didn't meet me at the library the next morning he told me to run." Pamela looked up at her husband and said, "I didn't come here to escape an abusive ex-boyfriend. I came because if I stayed in Aruba whoever killed Neil was going to kill me, too."

"Oh, my God," her husband said. "Why did you lie?"

"I was so scared. I didn't know what to do or if telling you the truth would get you killed, too. So I lied. You took me in. You made me feel safe. We were happy. I don't know. I guess I started to believe my lie because the truth was terrifying."

Her husband continued to hold her, but he was obviously struggling to accept that he didn't know his wife as well as he'd thought. "Do you know where this Kent Barrington is? If you do, tell them. I don't know what Neil did, but you need to help set it right."

Pamela looked down at the phone again. "He has his sister's eyes and his father's smile."

"What are you saying?" her husband demanded, shaking her.

Grant stood absolutely still, letting the scene play out. Viviana held her breath, afraid to do or say anything that would close the door to the truth.

Pamela walked over to a bureau and took an album out. She flipped it open, hugging it to her chest while running her hands over the photos in it. "Neil was paid to kill the baby, but he couldn't do it, so he brought the baby to me. I wanted him to take it back. All I could think about was how frantic his parents must be. Neil said we couldn't. He said there was a price on the child's head. If he didn't kill it, someone else would. I thought the baby belonged to a member of a gang or the Mafia. When I was on my way to the airport, the taxi driver told me there had been an accident and several people on the island had died. I knew I had to take the baby with me but I didn't have anywhere to go, so I came to you, Dave. I took a chance that you might still have feelings for me and you did. If I had known he had a family who was looking for him, a family who could keep him safe, I would have said something. But I was so afraid that if I ever went looking for answers, whoever killed my brother would kill him too. And maybe me and even you, Dave. I'm so sorry. I didn't know what else to do."

"Kade is the man they're looking for?" Dave asked.

She handed the album to Viviana. "I think so. He looks like them."

Viviana flipped through the album with Grant. She was about to ask him what he thought when she saw his eyes tear up. He wrapped an arm around Viv and hugged her tightly. "We found him, Viv." Then he tensed and looked up. "Tell me he's still alive."

Pamela sank into a chair. Dave hovered around her, looking lost as far as what to do. "He's very much alive. Dave legally adopted him when he was still an infant. He doesn't know. Oh, my God, we'll have to tell him."

"Call him now," Grant said in a cold tone. "We're not leaving without him."

Viviana saw horror fill Pamela's eyes. "You can't just throw this at him. He's my son. I'm the only mother he's ever known. I don't know what this will do to him."

Dave laid a hand on his wife's shoulder. "He has a right to know."

She looked up at him with fresh tears filling her eyes.

"Do you hate me? Will he? I fell in love with you and him and the life we made together. I wouldn't have lied to you if there was any other way."

"I want to believe that," Dave said with a sad smile.

With her heart breaking for everyone in the room, Viviana said, "Her version matches everything we know about what happened. Her brother was murdered. Anyone who had anything to do with taking Kent and switching him with another baby died within a short time." Viviana went to kneel in front of the broken woman. "You were right to run, right to hide. They would have killed you and Kent. Everything supports your fears. No one will hate you once they understand. You more than loved Kent, you saved him. He'll see that. Everyone will—even if they don't at first."

Dave remained still and silent.

Still holding the album, Grant crossed over and helped Viviana back to her feet. "I have to tell my family today. My mother has suffered too long over this. And as soon as my family knows Kent is here, they will come. You have a little over twenty-four hours to tell him or he'll find out from us." He met Dave's eyes. "I don't know how much of this story is true, but I do know how this will play out. If you run, I will find you. If you were anything but good to my brother or had anything to do with what happened to him, I will kill you. I assure you, whoever you thought might come for you would have given you a kinder, quicker death than I'll dole out if I discover a reason you deserve it. And, no, in case you're wondering, we're not here alone."

Viviana searched Grant's face for a hint that he was bluffing, but his cold eyes sent a shiver down her spine. Knowing the story as she did, she wasn't sure she could blame him, but she did send up a prayer that Pamela was not lying. She took his hand in hers and gave him a tug toward the door. "We're going to go now, but we'll be back tomorrow morning. Could you have Kent meet us here?"

Dave said, "His name is Kade. It's the only name he's ever known, but yes, we'll have him here tomorrow morning."

Pamela started to sob into her hands as Grant and Viviana exited the home. Grant looked calm but he was clutching the album so tightly his knuckles were white.

Viviana waited until they were in the car before she said, "You did it, Grant. You found Kent."

As he lowered his guard, he let his shock show. "We did it, Viv. You and me. I don't know if I will really believe it, though, until I see him. I wanted to demand to meet him right now, but if he has no idea he was adopted, maybe he needs to hear that part first from someone he trusts."

There he was, the man she loved with all her heart. A man who could put the needs of another before his own even in a situation where it must be tearing him apart.

"Do we call him Kade or Kent?" Grant asked.

"I don't know," Viviana said, taking his hand in hers again. "Maybe we let him decide."

"We have to tell the family. Holy shit, they're going to lose their minds."

"I have an idea," Viviana said when she realized she was still in possession of his phone. "Do you trust me?"

"One hundred percent."

She dialed Kenzi's husband, Dax, first and asked him to stay on hold while she merged the call. She scrolled through his contacts and one at a time added Emily, Willa, Helene, and Dale. Once they were all on the line Viviana said, "Grant and I need your help."

"With what?" Dax demanded.

"Anything," Emily said and the rest chimed in their agreement.

"We found Kent, and he's alive," Grant said.

"Oh, my God," Dale said.

"Where?" Dax barked.

"Bright, Australia. We're going to meet him for the first time tomorrow morning."

"Are you sure it's him?" Dale asked.

"He looks just like us, Dad. I'll send you photos of him. Once you see them you won't have any doubt."

"What do you need us to do?" Willa asked.

Viviana and Grant exchanged a look. She didn't need to tell him why she'd chosen who she had. He agreed. "This isn't something I could tell Mom and my siblings over the phone. You have all brought love and sanity to our family. I hate to put this on you, but could you tell everyone for us. They'll have questions that we can't answer yet, but get them on a plane and get them here; we'll figure this out together." He laced his hand with Viviana's. "Oh, and Viviana and I are engaged. Work that in however you feel is best."

"Welcome to the family," Dax said. "We need you."

Helene asked, "Who should tell Ian?"

"I will," Dale said. "I'll tell him."

"Okay," Grant said. "Thank you. Viviana and I are here if you need to talk more about it tonight."

Dale cleared his throat. "Grant."

"Yes, Dad?"

"I knew the moment you agreed to find Stiles you would bring us the answers. I never dared dream that you'd find Kent alive, but I don't doubt that you did. You have always been capable of doing the impossible when you set your mind to it. This time you achieved a miracle. Nothing short of a miracle. Thank you, Son."

Grant's eyes misted up, but he sounded composed. "You're welcome, Dad. It's not going to be easy, since Kent doesn't know us or even that he was stolen from us." He briefly outlined what Pamela had said had happened. "If she seems scared when you meet her, I did threaten her with a slow and painful death if I found out she was still lying."

"Let's hope she's not," Dax said. "Emily, do you want anyone to be there when you tell Asher?"

Emily sighed. "No. He'll run around like a chicken with his head cut off, but I'll hand him Joey, and that'll calm him down."

"And Andrew?" Dax asked.

"My parents are in town," Helene answered. "He gets along really well with my dad. He'll be fine."

"And Mom?" Grant asked. "I would be there if I could be."

"I'll tell her when we're alone," Dale said, "but then she'll want everyone there. How about a family meeting at our house first for dinner tonight?"

One by one they agreed then signed off.

Alone again in the car, Grant paused before starting the engine. "I might not have come here if you hadn't pushed me to."

She laid a hand on his chest and said, "Yes, you would have, because in here there is more than love, there is also a hero. My hero."

Epilogue

T HE NEXT MORNING, Grant and Viviana stepped out of their car onto the sidewalk in front of the Thompson home. From a distance, the man standing on the porch could have been Andrew or Ian. He was tall, ruggedly built and dressed in khaki shorts and a white T-shirt.

"He doesn't look happy to see us," Viviana whispered.

"I'm sure it's a shock," Grant said, trying to sound calm even though he had no idea what to say to a brother he was meeting for the first time.

Kent met them on the step, blocking their way inside. "You must be Grant. I googled the Barringtons last night."

"Hello, Kent."

"Kade," the man corrected. He came down another step. "Before this goes any further I need to set you straight on a few things. I am now fully informed about what happened in Aruba and why you're here. You need to know I've had a wonderful life. The people you threatened yesterday will always be my mom and dad. They have been the most caring, supportive, loving parents anyone could ask for. I appreciate that you all want to meet me, but it won't be done in a way that hurts them. Are we clear?"

Grant saw a little Asher in him as well, but in a good way. "I respect that, but you need to understand that while you didn't know about us we mourned for you. We never forgot you. Your real mother sees this as you being brought back to life. Take her feelings into consideration as well. Your twin might also be a little clingy. She has always held out the belief that you were alive."

In that moment, Grant glimpsed some of the confusion Kade was feeling. It was gone in a flash, replaced by the same stubborn look Kenzi often displayed. "Your mother birthed me. My mother saved me from killers. She sacrificed everything to protect me, and she never put that fear in me. She suffered silently and bravely. I don't know what you expect of me, but my life and my family is here."

Viviana stepped forward and said, "I lost my mother when I was eight. Now, you might not care about that because you don't yet care about me, but I spent my life longing for one mother. You have two. Two women who love you unconditionally. Sophie is a generous, kind woman, also. Let her into your life, let the Barringtons into your life. No one is asking you to choose, just open your heart and let more family in."

Grant nodded in approval. "What she said."

Kade's mouth twitched as if he almost smiled. "Do you sky dive?"

Grant shook his head. "No, but Andrew was a Marine. He'll jump out of anything at any speed."

"Do you surf?"

"No, but your twin Kenzi loves Jet Skis. She's an amazing swimmer as well."

"Hike?"

"I'm more of a treadmill warrior," Grant said.

This time Kade did smile. "So you wouldn't be interested in camping in the outback. There are places so vast you can see the curve of the earth, so open you'll see more stars than from anywhere else on the planet."

"That sounds like something you should get Lance to do, just don't let him hear any wild animals or he might swim home," Grant joked.

"That's awful," Viviana said with a smile. "Lance is a respected architect. Just because he is a little sweeter than the rest of you doesn't mean he wouldn't appreciate a good adventure. Not that he has time now that he has the twins. Oh, I hope he brings them and Willa. Kade, Pamela will love them. Those two little ones are adorable."

Kade nodded and seemed to relax. "How many people are coming over?"

Grant started naming his siblings, spouses, and their children. With each name, Kade's eyes widened more.

Viviana linked hands with Grant. "Technically, I will soon be family, too. We're getting married. Maybe here since everyone will be here. Wouldn't that be fun, Grant?"

"Fun," Grant said, swallowing hard.

Viviana slapped her forehead. "I'll start planning something. Oh, my God, I have to invite my dad and brothers. They are going to die when they hear where we are. My dad is excited that we're engaged, but he wants the wedding to happen before the baby comes. This would be perfect." She started to bounce with excitement. "Kade, my brothers would love to do everything you asked about. Do you mind if I call them now?"

Grant and Kade looked at each other, both at a loss for what to say in the face of her excitement.

For the next several minutes, Grant and Kade were a silent audience to a fast-paced feminine rundown of everything that had happened, along with an invitation to a wedding that had technically not yet been agreed to.

She put her phone on speakerphone. "Dad says they'll come. You have to hear how excited Dylan and Connor are."

"We're fucking going to Au-stray-lia," Dylan said. "I'm going to catch a kangaroo and name it something cool. Do you think they have them everywhere? Like you're walking down the street and bam one just walks by."

"They hop," Connor said. "Do you not know what a fucking kangaroo is? And I'm sure there are laws against catching them. Like the manatees in Florida. You can't molest them."

"I'm not going to kiss it. You're disgusting, Connor."

"That's what they call it when you bother a wild animal. Tell him, Dad."

"Maybe that's what they call what you do with wild animals, Connor," Dylan said.

"Shut the fuck up, Dylan."

"No, you shut up. If I want a kangaroo, I'm going to get a kangaroo."

Kade looked from Viviana to Grant and asked, "They're

really coming here?"

"Oh, they're even better in person," Grant said with a huge smile.

Thankfully, Viviana was too busy telling her family all about how they would probably fly over in a private plane. Grant hadn't thought it was possible to love her more, but when he saw Kade smiling as he listened to her, he fell in love with her all over again.

He had a feeling that was something he was destined to experience over and over. He would marry Viviana in Australia, Boston, or on the moon if that's what she wanted. No matter what the future brought, they would tackle it together—and she'd find a way to make him laugh while they conquered it.

THE END

Want to keep reading? Sign up here for my newsletter to be notified of the next release:

forms.aweber.com/form/58/1378607658.htm

Or check on my website at www.ruthcardello.com

Made in the USA
Middletown, DE
06 July 2022